When Polly bought back the old house of her childhood she intended to lead a quiet and tranquil life. She planted a garden and bought some dogs and settled down to enjoy the Suffolk countryside.

And then her sisters came – those ghosts from the past – and at the same time Dahlia, the girl who had helped Polly to make her fortune. And Dahlia, that vivid, unhappy creature of mixed background, was to disrupt the serenity of Pedlar's Green.

Also by Norah Lofts

JASSY
THE BRITTLE GLASS
A CALF FOR VENUS
QUEEN IN WAITING
SCENT OF CLOVES
THE LUTEPLAYER
BLESS THIS HOUSE
THE DEVIL IN CLEVELY
OUT OF THIS NETTLE
TO SEE A FINE LADY
THE ROAD TO REVELATION
HESTER ROON
MADSELIN
I MET A GYPSY
HERE WAS A MAN
BLOSSOM LIKE THE ROSE
WHITE HELL OF PITY
THE LOST QUEEN
HOW FAR TO BETHLEHEM?

The House Trilogy

THE TOWN HOUSE
THE HOUSE AT OLD VINE
THE HOUSE AT SUNSET

Norah Lofts writing as Peter Curtis

DEAD MARCH IN THREE KEYS
YOU'RE BEST ALONE
THE LITTLE WAX DOLL

and published by Corgi Books

Norah Lofts

Requiem for Idols

TRANSWORLD PUBLISHERS LTD
A National General Company

REQUIEM FOR IDOLS

A CORGI BOOK 0 552 08888 9

Originally published in Great Britain
by Methuen & Co. Ltd.

PRINTING HISTORY
Methuen edition published 1938
Corgi edition published 1972

This book is copyright. No portion of it may be reproduced by any process without written permission. All inquiries should be addressed to the publishers.

Condition of sale—This book is sold subject to the
condition that it shall not, by way of trade *or otherwise*,
be lent, re-sold, hired out or otherwise *circulated*
without the publisher's prior consent in any form of
binding or cover other than that in which it is published
*and without a similar condition including this condition
being imposed on the subsequent purchaser.*

This book is set in Monotype Baskerville

Corgi Books are published by Transworld Publishers Ltd.,
Cavendish House, 57–59 Uxbridge Road,
Ealing, London, W.5.
Made and printed in Great Britain by
Hunt Barnard Printing Ltd., Aylesbury, Bucks.

Contents

PART ONE *COMING* 9

PART TWO *GOING* 105

PART I
Coming

I

I CAME back to London in the third week of August at the tail end of a heat-wave. London was empty and smelt of dust and petrol. I realised how clever it was of Dahlia to delay her return for a week or two. I telephoned four people, one after the other. Three were away, and the fourth was just leaving for Denmark. 'Come too,' he said – he was a kind person – 'there's a good party of us, and it's God's chosen country at the moment.' I said, 'Thanks, but I'm only this minute back. I've got a lot to do. I'll be all right. I'll look into Monty's tonight, there'll surely be somebody there.'

But Monty's was empty, too, except for a few people up from the country. Not a soul I knew. And the coffee wasn't fit to drink. I went back to my hotel. The light was wrongly placed for reading in bed, and the chambermaid hadn't given me the third pillow I'd asked her for; and it was then, at that moment, that I made up my mind to get back to my flat, or failing that another – anything, anywhere so that I could be on my own.

And then next morning I went down Regent Street. It was a bright morning, though not so hot, and over the grey curve of stone there was the blue curve of the sky. I walked along looking at it, and quite suddenly nostalgia had me by the throat and I was madly planning a thing I should have scoffed at forty-eight hours before. I was going to have a house of my own, and it wasn't going to be in London.

I bought a paper and took it into the park, meaning to work straight through the lists of houses for sale. And then the miracle happened. From the place where it was humbly tucked away the name of the house leaped up at me, the first words I read on the whole of that page. And although it set my heart racing it left my mind untouched by anything but scorn for my own credulity. Even as my eyes flew over the rest of the advertisement I thought, after all the pedlars covered England in their journeys, and every village had a green, so there must be hundreds of Pedlar's Greens up and down the country. But by that time I had read the remaining lines and knew that this Pedlar's Green was indeed the one. 'Well, hell!' I said, and in my astonishment spoke aloud, for the woman at the other end of the seat looked at me sharply.

I folded the paper and tucked it under my arm and started up the path at a trot. In the street I waved frantically to a taxi-driver and gave him the house agent's address in a voice that shook. It isn't every day that you come up against a coincidence so startling as to seem miraculous. Within an hour I had made up my mind to buy a house in the country and been offered the one house of all others that I would have chosen, the house that I had left, blind with crying, eighteen years ago. I shouldn't have believed it if it had happened to any one else: I couldn't believe that it had happened to me.

Either my excitement or recent experience in America made the taxi seem dreadfully slow, and when at last I reached the place and explained my business the people seemed worse than slow, suspicious. They seemed to think that I ought to want to see it first and then proceed gently, step by step, to the business of buying. They were probably right. I hadn't seen the place for eighteen years; God knew what innovations had been made, what dilapidations had taken place in that time. But I wanted it to belong to me at once. I'm like that. If I want a thing I want it then and there. That is why I am so invariably badly dressed. I get up on a bright morning and think I want a thin frock. I go to a likely shop. There isn't one the colour I want; but the frock I like, and that fits me, can be made in that colour and delivered in a week. Hell, I think, and buy the right frock in the wrong colour. And since I do the same with shoes and hats and handbags, it's easy to see why I never have, and never shall have, anything approaching what they call an *ensemble*.

Anyway, I'd never bought a house before and wasn't familiar with the formalities.

'I'll give you a cheque now,' I told the man, 'and then I can start moving in today.'

He didn't seem to like the idea at all, and it occurred to me that perhaps he suspected my cheque.

'Would you like me to go and get the cash?'

He didn't jump at that either. By that time I was furious.

'Do you want to sell this house?' I asked him.

'Of course. Naturally.'

'Have you any reason for not wanting me to have it?'

'Of course not.'

'Then take this cheque and give me the keys.'

'But,' he said with the air of explaining something to a fractious child, 'the keys are not here. They're down at Little Swything – at the post office. Now if I give you an order to view . . .'

'All right,' I said, 'have it your own way. Only remember it's my house from now on. Nobody else is to step in and buy it while I'm trotting about viewing it.'

An acid smile came across his face.

'I don't *think* that there's any danger. Pedlar's Green has been for sale for over four years. That's why it's so cheap.'

I rushed around to the garage where, before I went away, I had left my car with instructions that it was to be kept in order and that Madge or Benny could use it as they wished. Both Madge and Benny were away – I knew that from my telephoning – so it would be there, and if it wasn't all ready for the road somebody was going to hear something. But it was; it was even clean. Benny always distrusts garages and says that garage men are the spiritual heirs of the horse-copers of an older day. But I have never found it so.

It was grand to order 'petrol' and to be understood. It was –

grand to have the familiar wheel in my hands. It was grand to go slipping along Hendon Way and to obey the sign that said, 'Fork right for St. Albans and the North'. Dear Suffolk, I haven't seen you in eighteen years and the harvest will be in your fields.

It was only August, and the sun was shining from a sky the colour of harebells, but the year was already menaced. There was no brightness in the green of the heavy foliage and the hard purple knapweeds were all that were left of the summer's wealth of flowers. But the passing of summer never saddened me, because I like the autumn.

I like the flare of colour in the trees, the asters and dahlias and sturdy zinnias on the barrows, and the autumn clothes in the shops. I like winter, too. It's a good season if you're properly fed and clothed and aren't hag-ridden as Penelope is, by the thought of people who are less fortunate.

Penelope is just a little mad. You often hear people say in praise of someone, 'He'd give you the coat off his back,' but Pen is the only person I've ever known literally to do it. She'd come up to London on business one bitterly cold day and we met and went to a matinée in the afternoon. She had a new coat for the occasion, the nicest coat she'd ever had, black, with some fur on the collar and down the front. When we came out of the theatre a woman who was selling heather or something like that appealed to us. I'd got used to passing such people without much thought in the days when every penny was important to me, but that afternoon I was in funds and feeling cheerful because of having had Pen to myself for a little while, so I fished out a half-crown, and knowing that Pen wouldn't have any money to spare, said out of the corner of my mouth, 'That's all right.' But Pen wouldn't come away. She put her hand in her pocket and brought out a return half-ticket, four stamps, and a shilling. She made a little face at them and then held them out to me. 'Hang on to these,' she said, and then and there, in the middle of the crowd coming out of the theatre, she took off the new coat and hung it over the woman's shoulders. Then she dashed away up the street with me behind her. The icy wind pressed the sleeves of her shabby blouse against her arms. 'You are a mad fool,' I said when I'd caught her. 'There was no need to do that. She'll only sell it; your nice new coat.'

'I don't give a damn what she does with it,' said Pen through her chattering teeth. 'She was *blue*.'

It was quite true. The woman was blue, and Pen wasn't far off being. I shoved her into a taxi and gave her a coat to go home in. I scolded a bit, too, until she shut me up by saying something that showed me a little of what went on inside her.

'It was cowardice, really, Polly. I'd so far rather be cold myself than have the agony of imagining what it must feel like to be so cold.'

'I see,' I said. 'But I'd a damn sight sooner have given her the one you have now and saved that new one.'

'You couldn't have been sure of finding her again,' Pen said simply.

I remembered that little episode, and thought, as I saw signs of summer's ending that day, that winter in the North, in a distressed area, must be pretty average hell for Penelope.

The car is a good one, not showy or streamlined; just a heavy powerful two-seater with its value in the engine, and when at last I turned off the road to the North there was plenty of room where she could stretch herself. It was still early in the afternoon when I slowed down to pass through Stoney Market, the ancient little gathering of houses and shops and schools that had always been 'town' to us. It looked very much the same, though there were traffic signals where the Haymarket crossed the Tollgate; and a new cinema, very smart in black stone and chromium, seemed to challenge the old Market Cross in the Square. I caught a glimpse of Mr Woolworth's peculiar brand of scarlet, too, as I drove past the end of the Pinnery.

Once out of Stoney I was in my own country, flat and

fertile, with low hawthorn hedges and great elm trees. The last of the corn was being carted and some of the trees by the roadside were hung with strands of wheat and barley that had brushed off as the loaded wagons passed beneath. My heart really raced with excitement. It was far more thrilling than seeing a pre-view of a picture that I'd had a hand in. When I caught sight of the square tower of Little Swything church peeping over the trees, I had trouble with my breathing.

I drew up at the post office and went into the little dark place that smelt of bacon and soap and tobacco and the leather of the heavy boots that hung in bunches like fruit awaiting the needs of a farm-labourer who still shopped at home.

'I believe,' I said to the fat woman, who moved with some difficulty in the narrow space behind the counter, 'that you have the keys to Pedlar's Green.'

'Well,' she said in a comfortably oiled voice, 'I did have. But it's so long since anybody asked for them. . . . I don't quite know. . . . I'll see.'

She fumbled about, rooting behind boxes and bottles and under papers. As the hunt grew more desperate she breathed harder and harder. I thought of an amiable pig in search of an edible root. But this waste of time did not, for some reason, annoy me like the house agent's hesitation had done. At last she said, unnecessarily, 'I don't seem to be able to lay my hands on them. I must think.'

She retired behind the post office end of the counter and held a meeting with herself. Very effective. Suddenly she said in a most relieved tone, 'I got it. They was the ones I put down our Fred's back time he had the nose bleed.' She disappeared through the doorway, and in a comparatively short time came back triumphant, and the cold iron met my impatient palm.

Front door, back door, side door. Familiar to me as my face: labelled in typed letters on dirty labels bearing the house agent's names. My God, anybody could have had them – our keys! Every night father had gone round and turned them in the locks. Or, if Penelope or Megan were going to be late (I was never late, being only a child then) the front-door key was laid in the candlestick on the chest in the hall to remind the late-comer to use it. You couldn't have carried it up in the candlestick, however absent-minded you might be; it was too heavy, a jailer's key almost. My key!

I thanked her quickly. Neither of us mentioned orders to view or anything about returning the keys. I ran out to the car and in a palsy of impatience turned into the lane that led to Pedlar's Green. Within five minutes I came to a standstill on the wide rough grass border that lay between its gate and the rutty lane.

I sat still for a moment, just looking at it. It was just like my memory of it but smaller, as things are to the adult eye. It was much overgrown, rather like the castle where the enchanted beauty had slept for a hundred years. The shrubbery had thickened enormously; I could see by the pallor of the leaves that the laurels hadn't been cut back for years, yet even now it looked far smaller and lighter than it had done in the old days when it had been my mental concept of a forest and I had imagined all sorts of terrors in its dusty depths. The eight poplars, four on either side the gate, still rose straight and slim, their heart-shaped leaves quivered so that as the undersides turned to expose their grey the whole tree seemed to change colour.

Beyond the poplars and the stretch of neglected garden stood the low house. The windows were almost completely overgrown with creeper just about to change colour, or with climbing rose sprays where the last frail buds were growing side by side with the withered remains of the flowers that had bloomed earlier in the year. There was moss on the thatch, that was itself riddled with sparrows' holes. Could anybody thatch in these days, I wondered; and to what extent had the neglect, so apparent from the outside, crept within?

I stepped out on to the overgrown grass border of the lane and laid my hand on the gate. It had once been painted white, but it was chipped and stained now, and the suns of several summers had raised blisters which had peeled off, leaving the naked wood exposed. I took out my little notebook and scribbled 'Paint'; that was the first thing. Gallons and gallons of paint, white wherever possible, and not too shiny. So I wrote it down. I intended to be very methodical. Method is a virtue that I admire very much because it makes life easier. Every New Year I made a resolution to be methodical, but the numerous muddles into which I floundered proved to me, repeatedly and clearly, that I hadn't yet attained the art. However, over each new piece of work I resolve again; so now, book in hand, I set out to survey my kingdom. Almost immediately I added, 'Catch to front gate,' for the catch and the mouldered wood that had held it had come off in my hand. The hinges weren't so good either, I reflected, for the gate had sunk, and as I pushed it inwards it scraped up a long velvety fold of moss that had gathered on the gravel. Amongst the tangled undergrowth of the garden there were a few vivid marigolds that had seeded themselves and looked as tough and wild as weeds.

I stepped on to the damp-greened doorstep and fitted the great key into the lock. It turned with a screech, the door stuck for a moment and then yielded. The musty scent of an old tree-surrounded house, long empty, met me. I sniffed at it. I found it neither disturbing nor depressing. It was indeed the right smell, the smell that there had always been in the cupboard under the stairs where we had kept our rubber boots and hoops and skates, and, later on, our hockey sticks. Racquets were never kept there because the damp rotted the gut. I remembered that the word 'gut' was only used once with reference to rackets – Mother objected to it strongly and always spoke of 'string'.

The house had altered very little. Somebody had put in electric light from the grid that crossed the fields at the back of the house, and some of the papers had been changed – not greatly for the better, I thought; but in eighteen years some of the back premises had not even received a coat of whitewash, and in the attic where we had sometimes played on wet days there were our heights marked on the wall and labelled with our names and the date: Penelope Millican Field, Megan Millican Field, Phyllis Millican Field. The pompous young signatures of Pen, Meg, and Polly. I looked at them with amusement. And the amusement surprised me a little. I had expected to feel – what? Sentiment? A wistfulness over the forgotten years? A yearning for the old family days? I don't know. Anyway, I felt none of them. I went around, filling my notebook and recognising things with pleasure and a certain feeling of excitement. I could imagine Madge saying, as she so often had done, 'Polly, you're so *hard*.' And my reply, 'You have to be, in this hard world.' And since no amount of yearning would bring back those days, since nothing will in Lamb's words 'ring the bells backward', I surveyed the house with eyes on the future, what I would make of it, how decorate and furnish, how gladly occupy it.

I opened every window, peeped into every cupboard, jumped on every squeaky board. Finally I climbed through the trapdoor to inspect the tank that supplied the bath. Then, warm and grimy, full of plans and utterly content, I sat down on the window-seat in the hall to smoke a cigarette and do a few sums in my head. In eighteen years I had had no place that I could rightly call 'home'. Other people's houses, grim lodgings, hotels of varying kinds, and a half share of a flat full of mirror glass, chromium plate, and scarlet leather, that was my record. God! What wouldn't I have here! Whiteness and space, dull surfaced walls and shiny wood, silver, thin china and fine linen, mirrors, cunningly placed, not just for show. The low, square, spacious rooms deserved all these, and so, I thought, did I.

I closed the windows again and locked the doors. Then I took the road to Stoney Market through the mellow afternoon, singing at the top of my untuneful voice. And that part of the day wasn't wasted either, for although only one person alive could have heard anything but noise in my singing, the tune was there and so were the words, and at night in the funny dark room at the pub I had chosen, before even I washed my hands, I scribbled the words and some marks that stood for accents on a piece of paper and set it aside for Dahlia.

II

PERHAPS I ought to explain about Dahlia straight away. In fact I owe her that, for if there had been no Dahlia I should never have owned Pedlar's Green, or a roadster, or a reliable watch, or, in fact, any of the things that I do. When I met Dahlia we were both utterly down and out. I had three pound notes and some loose silver, so I was better off than she was, though when you're out of a job and have no immediate prospects of anything but scullery work in front of you, there isn't much difference between three pounds odd and a half-crown, which was all she had. I had just bought a paper, intending to look for some kind of work; and as it was a sleety, windy day, I couldn't study it in the street, and, besides, I'd had no breakfast, so I turned into a grub-shop place that looked dim and dirty and cheap.

There wasn't a spare table – there never is in a really cheap place – so the waitress pushed me into a chair at a table where a girl was already sitting. She'd got a pot of tea in front of her, but she hadn't poured any out yet. She sat there staring at the streaming windows and she had the most desolate expression that I've ever seen on any face. I looked at her at first with that guarded kind of hostility that

English people show to strangers with whom they have to share feeding or travelling arrangements; and then I saw her misery and the fact that she was a half-caste, or a quadroon, or something of that kind, and my interest quickened. I don't know why, but any suggestion of a trace of exotic blood in anybody fascinates me straight away, so while I waited for my coffee to cool I watched her from behind my paper. I'd forgotten all about looking for a job – which perhaps explains my character. Father, who was very familiar with his Bible, once said that I would have been a good Athenian, always running after 'some new thing'.

This girl looked awfully cold, as well she might, for she was wearing a little black suit, which, though it had been good and was well cut, was completely inadequate for wearing on such a day. Her face was small, and to my eyes extremely attractive, thin, hollow, unhappy, and the colour of very milky coffee. Her eyebrows were narrow, very black, silky; and under them the great dark eyes with curiously blue-tinted whites stared out unseeing, oblivious even of me and my badly concealed interest. Except for an untidy strand or two her hair was pushed away out of sight beneath an ugly old felt hat. She had no handbag, and when at last she drew herself together and went to pick up the teapot that stood in front of her, I saw her loosen the clenched fingers of one bony little hand and move what she was holding into the other. A half-crown and a small dark bottle.

She took a sip of the unsweetened, milkless tea, gave a little shudder, and reached for the sugar basin. I counted the lumps. Six, and then another was seven. Very swiftly and slyly she pulled the cork out of the bottle and tipped the contents into the syrupy tea.

I think I am the least psychic person in the world. I seldom dream, never have premonitions or anything like that, but as the cork came with a squeak out of the neck of that bottle a cold trickle went down my back. I shrugged my shoulders to get rid of the feeling. Hell, I thought, am I getting so jumpy that the sight of a girl taking a tonic or any other dope she happens to fancy is going to set me imagining things? Not likely. But all the time I knew. Something far deeper and wiser than my shoulder-shrugging reason knew quite positively that she was up to no good. Her clothes, her face, that one coin in her hand, her furtiveness, were all assurances that I didn't really need. Just as she reached her hand out to lift the cup I swept my paper over the table. The milk jug went over, the cup tilted, seemed to rock for an instant, and then fell to the floor with a crash.

The girl drew in her breath with a hissing sound and looked at me with the whites of her eyes showing like those of a frightened horse. People at nearby tables looked up and a waitress with an air of poisonous patience came hurrying with a dirty cloth.

'I'm awfully sorry,' I said. 'Just like my clumsiness. You'll let me order you some more, won't you?'

She shook her head.

'I don't want any more, now,' she said; and her voice went to my heart. Deep it was, and velvety, with a sort of sob in it, just like the low note on a mellow violin. It was then, and is now, the loveliest voice I have ever had the fortune of hearing.

She put down the half-crown on the wet cloth and in one movement, it seemed, was out of her chair and at the shop door. I fumbled for a sixpence, threw it down, and followed her. The waitress yelped, 'Your ticket, miss. Pay at the desk,' but I waved my hand towards the table and rushed into the street. I caught hold of the girl by the elbow.

'Look here,' I said breathlessly, 'I dare say you think I'm clumsy and pushing, but I just couldn't help myself. I had to do it and I had to follow you.'

She jerked her elbow and stalked on without answering. In a minute we were in the crush of the Strand. Feeling more of a fool every second, I renewed my grip of her sharp elbow and managed to keep beside her at the cost of a few black looks from the people that our ill-directed progress jostled. Then I saw a few interested glances and realised that the girl was crying. We were just at the mouth of a little quiet street, almost a cul-de-sac, and I braced my feet on the pavement and swung her out of the crowd. Just ahead of us a man came through the swing door of a public-house and inside I could see, before the door closed on it, the glow of a red roaring fire.

'Do stop crying for a moment,' I said, holding out my handkerchief. 'Whatever it is, short of the police being after you, I can cope with, if you'll let me. Now come in here and let's have a drink and get warm.'

I'd completely forgotten that I was broke to the wide myself. Compared with this thin, sobbing, little coloured girl I felt big and solid and capable. I pushed the door with my shoulder and pulled her inside.

We were very lucky. All the men in the place but one were standing or perching on stools at the counter. The one who was warming his behind at the fire moved away when we sat down on the padded seat that ran along the wall by the fireplace. I pushed her along so that she was in the range of the outflung heat, and then I went to the counter and bought two double whiskies.

'Here you are, drink this,' I said; 'it's better than tea the way you make it, so now I don't owe you anything and you can snap out of it and tell me why you've spoilt my morning.'

'It was nothing to do with you.'

'True,' I said with a grin of embarrassment, 'but I didn't like the look of your medicine. Tell me, was it medicine?'

'Only in the sense that somebody said the axe was – a cure for all diseases.'

'I thought so. And what on earth do you want to do *that* for?'

'I can't see what it is to do with you,' she said stubbornly.

'Oh, nothing,' I said. 'Only you're young – and far too pretty to go out that way.'

She looked at me oddly.

'Women don't generally think other women pretty . . . or

bother about them if they are.'

I laughed.

'Wrong again,' I said. 'I'm not that sort. I interfered, I'll admit, and in return I'll do what I can to help you. God knows it mayn't be much, but we may as well try. Drink your dope and then tell me.'

She poured down the whisky as though it were water, and she thawed visibly in the heat of that wonderful fire, but it was a long time before she would talk. However, I stuck at her and by alternate coaxing and bullying managed to get the gist of it, at least. She'd been a singer – a good one, she said, and from hearing her speak I could believe it. She'd been brought over from Kingston by an agent of Joe Tolly, whose boast is, as you know, that he rakes the world for talent. She'd starred in three shows, none of which I'd seen, of course, and then she'd caught diptheria. They'd had to perform tracheotomy to save her life, and when she was well again her singing voice was gone. She'd saved a little, not much, but something, and instead of hopping off home she'd hung about looking for work, which, as I knew, was scarce enough when you were white and had references and things. Down to rock bottom at last, and turned out of her room, she had been all ready to cash in when I knocked her cup over.

'Hell,' I said, when I'd mastered the story. 'Why kill yourself? Plenty of people waiting to do that for you. Big buses and things. What you've got to do, with little encouragement and in the face of opposition, is to keep yourself alive. I'd go on the streets before I'd kill myself.'

Dahlia (she'd told me her name) shuddered. 'I couldn't do that,' she said.

'Well, I haven't any great fancy for it myself. I've done all kinds of things, but not that, yet. As a matter of fact I was just going to look up advertisements for parlourmaids and cook-housekeepers, though I cook like the devil. I don't think you'd quite do for that kind of thing, you're too decorative. What can you do?'

'Nothing, except with music. Once I got a job playing at a cinema. But they got a gramophone thing and didn't want us any more. Always it's like that. Not wanted.'

She looked at me with those great tragic eyes, and suddenly, just like that, my brilliant idea took birth.

'Look here,' I said, 'how musical *are* you?'

'Very musical,' she said simply.

'Can you write it?' She nodded. 'I mean can you put down on that lined paper stuff notes that you've never seen, only heard?'

'Of course.'

'Almighty God!' I said. Then I dropped my head in my hands and stared at the red cave of fire and I thought – if only it worked! God!

I made songs, you see. I'd been making songs since before I left school. The words would come into my head and I could hear the tune that came with them. It was there, whole and fitting, but I might just as well have tried to show somebody my left lung as to try to make another person know what the tune was. I just couldn't understand music, read it, or write it or even sing properly. And so there I was with a thousand songs in me, doomed to eternal silence so far as I could ever see. But now . . .

I tore the woolly scarf from my neck and wrapped it twice round Dahlia's, tucking the ends down like a bib inside her flimsy coat.

'Come on,' I said. 'I once heard a joke about Mr Derry meeting with his Tom, but that is nothing to this meeting if you're as good as I think I am.'

I stopped at three shops. At one I bought the smallest quantity of lined paper that they would sell me; at the next four of the largest ham sandwiches they could cut; at the third a packet of cigarettes and some matches. I'd given up smoking weeks before, but now I felt that inspiration must have its incense. Then I found a piano shop that let off rooms for practise, and hired one till six, when the shop shut. At ten minutes to six we staggered out of the place, blind and almost dumb with concentrated effort. The paper was full of the funny little squiggles that Dahlia had made with my fountain-pen: seven songs of the best.

It was still sleeting, and, Lord! I felt I wanted to pick her up and carry her to my room, she was so precious - wizard means nothing; genuis doesn't touch it. I'd just sit down and say, 'Now this song is called "The world Is Too Much For Me". It's kind of half mocking and half serious, if you can understand that, and it goes like this.'

Then, in my quite tuneless voice, I'd chant it to her, bringing out the words clearly and emphasising the beat as I could hear it. And she'd fiddle about and strike odd notes with her head on one side as though she were listening to something that I couldn't hear. Then, presently, she'd play it through and I'd say, 'Faster,' or 'Slower,' or 'A shade higher there.' And suddenly it was all complete – just as it had always been in my dumb head. When she said at last, 'I only wish I could sing some of these. I never had a song half so good,' I was almost choked with excitement. So, humming and tinkling and scribbling, we got down seven songs before the shop closed; and then I took Dahlia home with me.

That evening I sent the manuscripts off. I knew exactly what to do with them, because I'd so often thought about what I would do if ever I learned to understand and write music. Only, of course, I never could have learned.

And now that I had cast upon the waters some bread that might conceivably return to me buttered, I gathered enough courage, or rather face, to write to Penelope, to ask her for a loan. She sent me ten pounds like a lamb, though heaven alone knew how she raised it, kept the room for us and bought us bread and coffee until somebody realised that the stuff was good, and after that it was just like a fairy-tale.

A successful song can bring in the money quicker than almost anything. It has so many angles. And I'd been making songs for so long that I had a great stock. Besides, now that the dumbness had lifted I could see a song in the slightest incident. They came flocking. I happened, for instance, to say to Dahlia, 'You're my mascot. You're what I've been wanting all my life.' And there it was, the germ of the biggest song hit of a decade. As easy as that.

My name being Phyllis and Dahlia's being what it is, we put the two together and called ourselves 'Phyllida'; and if you will notice the window of any music-shop, or study a list of records of popular songs, and remember that we did all the songs for *Yesterday Calling* and *Sigh No More*, and had got our hooks into the film-song world as well, you will understand why I could buy Pedlar's Green and have it fit to live in in three weeks.

You will understand, too, perhaps, why I have given Dahlia the first place here.

III

For three weeks the house was full of men – plumbers and electricians, plasterers and painters. It was like a human ant-heap, and in the middle of the proceedings the whole thing looked such a muddle that I was seized with despair. I wandered about with no place to sit, I trod on wires and tripped over paint-tins – obviously a nuisance whose sole purpose was to make and serve out gallons of tea from water heated on an ill-disposed oil-stove. I removed myself at last and set out in search of furniture.

And it wasn't until then that I had any idea at all of reconstructing my home as I had known it. I ought to make quite clear – indeed, to emphasise that point – the past was finished, so far as I was concerned. I'd been happy there in the way that children are happy. I'd had enough to eat and wear, I had liked both my sisters and loved one. Mother's intimidating manner had not distressed, nor Father's otherworld inefficiency irritated me as they would have done had I met with them later in life. But I didn't in the least mind altering the house or cutting down a tree or two in the overgrown garden. And I meant to buy all new furniture. Not chromium plate and scarlet leather. I'd had enough of that; but new stuff, solid and comfortable.

I went to shop after shop. I bought china and glass and cutlery. I 'considered' dozens of different tables and chairs and beds. None pleased me. One day I drifted, almost by accident, into a second-hand and antique furniture shop, and there suddenly I was at home. A black old dresser, a bow-fronted chest, a rosewood dining-table with thin brass splints to strengthen its corners, a grandfather clock, made in Colchester in 1692, two dower chests, a pew-like seat that might have been torn from church or inn – these took more money than I had expected to spend on all my stuff. But I had to have them, and when I found a work-table with a faded green silk bag hanging down like a dropped stomach and claimed that for my own, I realised that these were all things whose very close relations, at least, had stood in the rooms when I was a child. The hunt was on.

Every day I went out with unabated greed, and my store in the barn grew daily, as though every day a fresh grandmother had died and left me all her household goods. I avoided, I hope, the obvious and the ugly, though I did admit a reproduction if it were made with care and skill. I enjoyed that shopping. I met some curious people, too: old men mostly, with odd interesting bits of historical knowledge tucked away in their unprepossessing and often rather dirty heads.

When I gave my attention to the house again it was miraculously clear and calm. The lights and the stoves and the handles worked, the doors and windows opened easily and closed securely, the white paint shone, the rough white paper was ready to be an unobtrusive and flattering background for my findings, the dark stain lay ready for my coloured rugs. Help, that was the next thing.

The last maid we had had there, the one who had been trained by Mother and had remained to look after Father and me, had been a girl named Agnes, a big, fresh-coloured youngster with a crop of freckles and carroty hair. Her home was in the village, and I thought that I would begin by calling there and asking Mrs Porter, Agnes's mother, if she knew any one who would at least help me move in.

Mrs. Porter, whom I dimly remembered, came, as I thought, to the door. It was ridiculous, of course, but I had forgotten those eighteen years.

I addressed the woman as Mrs Porter. I was aware of a certain stiffening, and she said codly:

'I'm Mrs Turner. My mother, as was Mrs Porter, has been dead five years.'

I looked rather more closely, and then, greatly daring, said, 'Agnes. I don't suppose you remember me, do you? Phyllis Field. I used to live at Pedlar's Green, and I've come back.'

'No, I shouldn't have known you.'

'You've altered, too, I said foolishly.

There was an awkward kind of silence. A bit haltingly, in the face of Agnes's unmoving expression, I explained what I had come for.

'Only for the move?'

'Well, really, I want somebody who can cook a bit. There'll only be myself, most of the time, anyway.'

'I'll come,' said Agnes, still without a glimmer of expression. 'I'm looking for a job – only, there's the boy; most people 'on't have him.'

Your little boy?'

Agnes nodded. 'He ain't so little, he's five and he's quiet, only people 'on't believe it.'

'I don't mind a bit. And he needn't be so quiet, there's plenty of room there, as you know.'

'Answer to prayer, this is,' said Agnes, without joy. 'Cissie and me had a set-to this morning. She don't want me here, and I don't want to be here. Shall we come now?'

I looked at my watch. It was almost noon.

'Yes,' I said, 'we can get the beds set up and so on. I've got a couple of men moving stuff in now. Shall I wait and drive you up?'

'Yes,' said Agnes. She turned into the house, leaving the door open, and I went to sit in the car. Voices reached me. '. . . going now this minute. Told you I would.'

'Taking your bastard with you, I hope.'

A tumult of shouts. Cissie? The younger sister who used to carry washing. Bastard? Only by courtesy 'Mrs Turner' then. Dear, dear Agnes! And how awful for the little boy, who would soon notice what names he was called. A crude people. In a surprisingly short time Agnes reappeared, a bulging wicker dress-basket with a strap round its middle in one hand, with the other dragging a small, doleful-looking little boy with a cropped head of almost white hair, and prominent teeth.

'Tommy,' said Agnes, by way of introduction.

I smiled at him and said, 'Hullo Tommy', but no answering smile appeared on the small face. He looked at me stonily and allowed himself to be seated upon his mother's rather inhospitable-looking lap. A pathetic, unwanted scrap of humanity, I thought, wronging Agnes, who, I later discovered, loved him with a fierce if rather uncomfortable love.

Agnes only volunteered one remark to me in the course of the hours that we worked together. The improvements that I pointed out to her with rather childish pride elicited no more than a grunt, whether of approval or the reverse I couldn't have said; but when I came across from the barn with the work-table clutched to my stomach the stony expression of her face just cracked a trifle, as she said, 'That always stood in your ma's bedroom.' I did not tell her that it was not, to my knowledge, the same. It might have been.

I brooded a little over Agnes as I ate my supper of eggs

and bacon, cooked on my own stove, at my own table. What had happened to turn that big, cheerful, raucous, grinning girl into this dumb and doleful woman? Was it simply what the village would call 'her trouble', or was it natural development? I thought of the number of times that Mother had had to rebuke her for singing so loudly in the kitchen that the whole house was disturbed, and sighed a little. Mother would so much have preferred 'Mrs Turner', and I would rather have had Agnes.

It was a mild evening, so mild that one was acutely conscious of the early darkening. I wandered out into the garden, the spark of my lighted cigarette going before me, and I thought of bulbs in hundreds, and of flowering shrubs that would bloom, one after the other, from March to August. Daphne first, flowering before the first leaf unfolded, pink almond, prunus, lilac, laburnum, syringa, hydrangea, fuchsia, and buddleia. Roses in the June twilights opening their hearts. I think I touched the peak of existence that night. The freshness and the accomplishment of beauty within awaiting me, and the promise without.

And I was young – though I didn't think consciously of that at that moment, and I'd been very lucky. My windows, lighted and uncurtained, shone for me. I thought, 'I have lighted a hearth.' I hadn't exactly, but I thought of it. And I twisted other words round the thought. It would make a song. Only, of course, it would have to be '*We* have lighted a hearth', and then it would appeal to all the couples who *had* got some sort of a home of their own, and it would wring the hearts of all the people who wanted one. In short, it would be a popular song. Toying with it, I went in at the kitchen way.

'Tommy asleep?' I asked conversationally.

'Yes. He go to bed early,' said Agnes.

'Well, I hope you'll both be happy here.'

'I hope so.'

Not a spark, not a spark. Agnes didn't like me. I thought, but dismissed the idea as imagination, that her eye fell disapprovingly on my cigarette. A few days later when Agnes broke silence to mention Mother, and ended, 'She was a lady, your ma was,' I understood it all. I had fallen short of the standard that Mrs Field's daughter should have measured to. I smoked, I drank, I swore, I wore pyjamas. *O tempora, O mores!*

Except for Agnes, whom I could have wished more cheerful, but who was an excellent cook (gloomy people often are, most surprisingly) and a willing servant, I was perfectly, almost idiotically, happy at Pedlar's Green for a whole month. There were still things to buy. I bought four dogs. After eighteen years of frustration I could indulge my passion for dogs. Method failed me again there. I meant to buy only recognised kinds, and began with a Scotch terrier, called Block, and a little smooth dachshund with an unpronounceable name which I altered to Velvet. Then one day, going through the market at Stoney, I saw two little pups in a cage. It was a warm day, one of those that come suddenly in September to remind one of Keats' 'Ode to Autumn'. Their tongues were hanging out; they had no water in the cage; and some children were trying to poke them out of their lethargy with sticks. I bought the pair for seven and sixpence. They were both mongrels, but I didn't really mind, because it was so fascinating to see a collie tail wave from a whippet hindquarters, and a spaniel's curly ears frame a long greyhound face. One was a bitch, and I did have some misgivings about what the third and fourth generations would look like after the two pedigree gentlemen had added their quota, but the time for bothering about that hadn't yet arrived. They were all very happy, and so was I.

It was lovely to wake in the white-walled, beamed bedroom and lie looking at the dark edges of the copper beech against the pale sky, waiting for Agnes to come up with the tea. She would open the door, and a flood, it seemed, of dogs would come pouring in, all bright eyes and wet noses and waving tails. I would give them biscuits out of the tin that I kept on a shelf near by. I drank my tea, bathed, and dressed in easy stages, playing with the dogs, looking out of the window, reading an odd page of my book, jotting down a line for a song. After breakfast I took the dogs out into the fields. The blackberries were ripe and shone richly black against their reddening leaves. Block would sometimes sight a rabbit and set off after it, looking like a cut-down rocking-horse in motion. The others followed. They never caught anything. After that I got the car out and went into the town, or drove idly through little-used country lanes.

Evening came all too soon, and at that season there was a bloom on it as there is on a grape. Sometimes after dinner I walked again, or saw a picture at the little cinema in Stoney. I like pictures, even bad ones offer you something. Sometimes I stayed in and read or played my gramophone.

It sounds a dull life, but to me it was delightful. To be able to do just what I liked, when I liked; to be able to have the kind of food I wanted, not the sort that some one else had chosen; to be able to arrange my own flowers even – to me these were all poignant pleasures. I fed fat my ancient grudge against penury and exile.

But there came an evening, the kind that every recluse must know, when I yearned for some one to talk to. It was a coldish evening and I held a match to the fire and drew the curtains. There was a nagging wind, too, that flung handfuls of brittle leaves against the windows. I thought, tonight I will indulge my shameful taste for hackneyed music. I opened my gramophone, and then, ignoring my new records, went upstairs for my old ones. I fished out 'Valse Triste', 'Finlandia', and 'The Lute Player', my old, and much begibed favourites.

Every single one was cracked. I swore. I felt just like a hungry person who has been offered a savoury dish, tasted it in anticipation, and had it snatched away. 'Finlandia' had the slightest crack, and I put it on, determined to ignore the little recurrent click. Music without words to me is a dead thing, and though I had fitted some of my own to 'Valse

Triste', I had chosen Humbert Wolfe's 'You, too, at midnight, suddenly awakening', for 'Finlandia'. 'The Lute Player' had its own.

An orgy, deliberate and self-imposed, of sentiment.

> You, too, at midnight, suddenly awakening,
>   May wonder, if you hear a step outside,
> Until your heart replies, what set it aching;
>   And listen knowing that your heart has lied.

I was just thinking, my God, this is a mistake. I haven't gone through this since . . . when the lid of the gramophone, insecurely poised, crashed down. Bits of poor 'Finlandia' spattered out over the floor and the rest grated together as the table of the machine went on revolving.

I said 'Hell!' and burst out laughing. It served me right. It was the best thing that could have happened. God bless that gramophone! I picked up the pieces and dropped them into the waste-paper basket. I held 'The Lute Player' and 'Valse Triste', one in either hand, and smote them together so that their fragments followed the others. So perish all traitors!

A good absorbing job, I told myself, is what you want. And there was one to hand. I had not yet written to either of my sisters to tell them the news about the house. I replenished the fire, filled my fountain-pen, hunted out the last letters I had received from them, sent actually for my birthday, and settled down to strengthen family ties and issue invitations.

They had always been known as 'the girls'. 'The girls are coming home tomorrow,' 'The girls want half a crown each for a subscription,' 'The girls send their love to you, Polly.' Pen was a little over eight when I was born, and Megan was nearly seven. They were, quiet literally, gods to me, Penelope especially. How far that was due to premature insight into a really sterling character, and how far due to the fact that even Mother seldom found fault with Pen, I cannot say. Now that we were all grown up, and past our first youth at that, the eight and seven years between us made little difference, but when we were children the gulf was wide and deep. They were always very good to me, and in many ways I profited in the early years by being the last of the family. Privileges that had cost them bitter struggles to attain, our mother being very old-fashioned, fell to me by right of custom; and I inherited their outgrown clothes and sports gear without having the cost thrown up at me as they had.

Penelope was clever: one of my earliest recollections is of being taken, all tortured curls and starch, into the town to the school's annual prize-giving, and seeing her, with her black legs quivering and her long plaits slapping her thin back, mount the platform to receive a pile of books in their shining presentation covers. Not until I was older did I appreciate the sheer drive and force that carried her, in those pre-war days, from a small remote farm to a university degree. And until one had appreciated the cost of her progress it was impossible to gauge the force of conviction that had made her throw it all away and give her life to the service of the Mary Montague Settlement in that grim northern town. How Mother would have grumbled about waste and folly had she ever known of it: but Mother was dead by then. Not, of course, that even Mother could have deterred Pen from doing what she wanted.

From a distance I had adored her, but since the break-up of our home I had seen remarkably little of her. She had come home from Oxford for Father's funeral with her face in bandages and hands that shook when she tried to pick up or reach out for anything. There was a mystery that I was not allowed to share, I knew that. I'd heard talk of an accident, and of an inquest, but my aunt who was my father's sister, and our only living relative and who had come to Pedlar's Green when he was taken fatally ill, had hidden the paper from me for over a week and had snubbed me brutally when I asked what kind of accident it had been. I meant to ask Pen, but my aunt asked first, and Pen had said in such a final way, 'I prefer not to talk about it,' that my own question was never asked.

After the funeral she and my aunt had had a long talk, to which I had listened from outside the door, since I knew that it was about me and I was anxious to know my fate. Pen had offered to leave Oxford, find a job and keep me. I stood outside the door and breathlessly prayed that she would be allowed to carry out this plan. I was only twelve and didn't realise what the offer meant in the way of sacrifice. And I hated my aunt. The month or so that she had spent at Pedlar's Green had been enough to assure me that we were never intended to live together. But Father, it appeared, had made other arrangements, almost the only ones he had ever made in his life, I should think. He had left enough for Pen to finish at college, and the rest, together with what the farm and the things on it fetched, was to go to my aunt to support me until I was sixteen and could, presumably, fend for myself. And since the will of the dead is sacred, however ineffectual the living person has been, Pen was overridden. Incidentally, Aunt Ada had taken a very bad bargain about which I did not fail to hear; I was glad enough of my first job when I was fourteen. And that had set me at a further disadvantage with Penelope, for, compared with her, I always felt ill-educated, raw and crude, as well as a defective character. And I knew only too well that if I had had a degree I wouldn't have spent my time in working for a pittance in the name of charity; I'd have been looking out for Polly Field.

I never wrote in my letters to Pen of how much I hated the feeling of dependence upon Aunt Ada, and of having to be meek and polite in the face of insult because of that dependence. And since I couldn't write about the things that were in the forefront of my young mind I had written very little to Pen at all. I had worked and drifted, and fallen down and got up again on my own. The ten pounds on the day I met Dahlia was the only thing I'd ever asked her for in my life. Since then we had met once or twice in

London, and we exchanged letters at long and irregular intervals.

Megan, my other sister, was as different from Pen as possible. Curious tribute to heredity lay somewhere there, for they had been born of the same parents, fed on the same food, slept for years in the same bed, attended the same school. And no two people on the face of the earth were less like one another. Megan was pretty, very pretty, Ever since I could remember she had been referred to as 'your pretty sister'. Megan had made me beauty-conscious. It used to be such a mystery to me. I used to look at Pen's face, then at Megan's, and then sometimes at my own reflection and think – what *makes* the difference? Two eyes, a nose, a mouth, some skin, features that individually even resembled one another, why was one arrangement so pleasing that every one remarked it, and another so commonplace? They were both fair, but Meg's hair verged on the golden, Pen's on the drab. Mine was plain brown. Meg's hair was prettier, I could see that, because of the colour and the curliness, but Pen's eyes were far more definitely blue. I used to go over them, feature by feature, like that, but the secret always eluded me.

I was about ten then, and ignorant. I didn't understand that quite a lot of Meg's advantage over Pen in appearance was due to her determination to exploit what she had in order to make up for her mental inferiority, or how much, again, her attractiveness lay in her gestures, her grace, her poise her complete confidence that she was pleasing. Pen could have competed far more if she had ever bothered. But, then, I *did* bother; I tried to copy Megan's looks, just as I tried to imitate Pen's cleverness, and with equal lack of success. Indeed, I laid a pretty foundation for a nice little inferiority complex, had I known about such things then. I used to copy Megan's style of hairdressing, her way of tying a ribbon, the angle at which she held her head when she was asking a favour. Useless. I was so much bigger of bone than either of them, my eyes didn't pretend to be blue, my feet grew so that I couldn't wear the shoes they had outgrown; I was clumsy and I was not clever. What hope had I?

And yet, I thought, brooding over my letters on this late September evening, it was 'poor Polly' who had made money with her unclever head and managed to secure a lover or two for her undistinguished body. That line of thought closed abruptly – it was neither seemly nor safe. I thought about Megan instead.

She had married immediately after the war. With some quibbling over her age she'd got into a hospital where her lyrical beauty had probably compensated for her lack of other qualities more usually associated with 'good works'. Henry her husband was a coffee planter, and they'd been in Kenya since nineteen-twenty. During their visits home I had seen her occasionally, but not much, for with her I had been ashamed of my clothes and general lack of sophistication. She sometimes sent me a cheque for a present in the old days, but I always felt it was Henry's money, and I didn't like Henry much; so if I was in a job I tore up the cheques and Megan never seemed to notice. In that way she was just like Father, who would read a pamphlet when he should have been at market or buy a first edition of some quite worthless book when what he needed was horse pills. Over money, dates, time, and tickets, Megan was as vague as only a beautiful woman can afford to be. Over other things, such as clothes, fashion, make-up, and current funny stories she showed a compensating practicality. I re-read their last letters.

Neither of the letters had reached me on my birthday, though both were written for that. Pen's was two days late and Meg's more than a fortnight. Tonight, reading them together for the first time, I was struck by a similarity between them. Penelope had written her good wishes and explained why she had no present for me, and added in the clear small writing that was so like her clear dry speech:

'This is, I'm afraid, a dull letter, and I know it will be late. I was up all last night, and I must admit that sometimes this place and the work here depress me rather. "Depressed" rather than "distressed" area, though God knows it's that, too. Last night we were with a woman, slaving to bring alive into this world that doesn't want it, the eleventh child of an unemployed miner and his consumptive wife. Kay – she's the doctor, and a fine woman – said she was in two minds about smothering it, and honestly it would have been much the kindest thing.

'Oh dear, Polly, wouldn't it be grand to be happy kids again at dear old Pedlar's Green? I often think of it. Can you remember it at all? How we used to gather those peach-scented oxlips in Galley Wood, and blackberry in the brakes? And we knew nothing of other people's troubles. You probably wouldn't go back. You've made a success of your life, and you're still young. So here's to another year; may it bring you more success and prolong your youth. . . .'

Megan's was quite different, naturally.

'How I envy you being only thirty, it's the best, the very best time of a woman's life. Young enough, old enough; just perfect. What wouldn't I give for it back again. Life is very cruel to women, I always think, Polly, and I tell you this so that you can make the most of your time. One wrinkle, a little sagging, a few grey hairs, and you're finished. What was that thing Father used to quote, "Not all your something and your wit can something it back," I often think of that. I wake up looking a fright; and then I long, I can't tell you how much, to be waking up in that back bedroom with Pen, seeing myself in that blurry little glass, tumbled and sleepy-eyed – but not a hag. Where does it go, that youngness?

'Perhaps you'll do better; anyway, don't think that you'll be a fright at thirty-seven, this climate is not kind. And you're only thirty, lucky Polly. I hope the songs are doing well; I've almost worn out the record of "Heart, be Content". It's a lovely thing and I love it. What an egoistic – or should it be egotistic? – anyway, what a beastly letter for your birthday.'

Of the two, I think I pitied Megan more. Perhaps I was wrong. But it seemed to me that every day Pen did something to alleviate the conditions that depressed her, whereas Megan, who had relied entirely upon her looks, was helpless in the face of their betrayal.

Anyway, I thought, as I stamped the envelopes of the letters I had written, they could both assuage their nostalgia, not for youth, but for Pedlar's Green. How surprised they'd be when they looked at the address of my handsome paper. They'd be certain to look at the address first; I had changed mine so often. They would know that I had come home.

Walking to the post-box that hung on a telephone post just beyond the mouth of the lane, I was filled with most unusual faintly melancholy abstract thoughts. Home, I thought, what we are all in search of. For Pen it would be a place where things were orderly and fair and just a trifle antiseptic in flavour. Megan would only find hers in a world where beauty lay beyond the hand of time. I, lacking alike ideals and beauty, could lay my hand on my home, tangible possessions, house, food, money, dogs. Without regret I reflected that I had what the Bible called a carnal mind. Outside I did not mind the wind, it seemed to bring the scent of bonfires and fallen apples and just a hint of frost. I dropped in the letters. One would go to the grimy house that was the M.M.'s headquarters, and in the cheerless hall be stuck in the rack under 'F'. The other would emerge into the sunshine of Africa, and Meg would receive it from a black hand.

I hoped that Pen would come before the colour had all gone from the countryside. Then if Megan took notice of my invitation and came in the spring, so that she missed the African summer, Pen could come again and so get two holidays. We'd all be together, and we could talk a lot and eat a lot, and try on one another's hats, and remember things and sit about munching the apples that had steadily ripened, even while the house was empty, and were now stored in the attic. It would be grand, I thought, to be all together at Pedlar's Green.

Hell, they say, is paved with good intentions. Merry, merry hell.

Pen's letter came within a week.

'Dear Polly, – Your letter was a surprise. I noticed the postmark at once and thought I was dreaming, then when I saw the address I felt delirious. What a wonderful coincidence, your seeing it like that, and how nice your description of it sounds.

'Have you heard or seen anything of Meg? I had a telegram ten days ago saying that she was in London, since then not a word. Henry is not with her. The telegram cost two shillings – isn't that just like her? Two shillings to whet one's curiosity and not a penny-ha'penny to allay it.

'It's nice of you to ask me to stay with you. One day I will; perhaps next summer. We're never so busy in the summer. Now we are, terribly. We've just started the children's meals again at the M.M. and we aren't sure of enough money to carry on to Christmas even. If people could only see the poor brats' faces I don't think there'd be a pet dog or a racehorse in England by the New Year. And yet I don't know. They must *know* and hear about work like this and the necessity for it. Oh, Lord, here I am, off again: but, having started, I may as well conclude – drop us a shekel or two if you've got a spare one. After all, we're very faithful to your "You're My Mascot" song. At least two people in the settlement can be guaranteed to be singing it at any one of eighteen hours. Did I say thank you for asking me? If not, thank you.

'Pen.'

She hadn't had a holiday to my knowledge for five years and then it was a seaside camp with a pack of children. She could have come if she'd wanted to. That was what her talk of longing for dear old Pedlar's Green amounted to. It reminded me of a play I once saw in which some women were always longing to go somewhere – Moscow, I think it was – and never did a thing about getting there.

And Megan was somewhere undefined in London while my letter went ramping out to Kenya. Well, hell, I thought, I can do without either of them. Dahlia had been in London for a month by that time; she'd be ready for something different. I went out to send her a telegram. She'd come, if only for free board. Poverty hadn't taught Dahlia to save her money. She was always very hard up.

Next morning, guided by the kind fate which looks after idiots and drunks, I was filled with the idea of getting extra help into the house. Why I thought of it I don't know; Agnes was perfectly capable of looking after two people. Perhaps I was afraid to face her with the news of a possible guest without an offer of help to soften the blow.

'There'll be another person to cook for,' I explained. 'Do you know any one who would come and help with the cleaning?'

'No, I don't know anybody.'

'Oh, Agnes, think,' I said. 'After all, it's for your convenience. There'll be two of us, and probably more later on' (I could think of at least eight people who would be glad of a nice quiet time in the country), 'and we mustn't entirely overlook Tommy, he has some claim on your attention.'

'There ain't no need to mention him. He come last,' said Agnes with a bitter note in her voice.

'But he shouldn't,' I persisted. 'That's what I mean. I don't want you to be driven and bothered. Think of some one who could come in for just an hour or two.'

Agnes said nothing. Oh, Agnes, my mind cried, be a little human, try to make life a little happy for yourself. Why make whatever it is worse with all this stubbornness?'

'You can't think of any one? Then I must ask at the post office.' I got down off the table where I was perching, and Agnes, with a swift look at me, said,

'There's Mrs Pawsey.'

'Mrs Pawsey? You don't mean our Mrs Pawsey, the one who used to help Mother sometimes.'

'The same.'

Mrs Pawsey had seemed old to me all those years ago. I was surprised to hear that she was still alive.

'She must be very old.'

'She's sixty-nine, but she's active,' said Agnes reprovingly.

'Do you think she would come?'

'I'd rather have her than anybody,' said Agnes, not exactly in answer. I was so much annoyed that I wouldn't even ask if the old lady still lived in the same house. I could find out.

Why Agnes even half approved of Mrs Pawsey was a mystery, for she was a garrulous old woman, who, in the course of ten minutes' conversation gave me a vivid synopsis of the history of the whole village during the eighteen years I had been absent.

'That Mrs Pamment now – oh, you must remember Mrs Pamment – your ma used to give her some of you children's clothes. You don't remember? Well, no matter, makes no difference, but as I was saying, she –' and so on.

Agnes's story came out, of course. 'Bad thing that was. Aggie Porter was a decent mawther. An' of course, coming back and calling herself "Mrs" didn't do her no good, not with that Cissie's tongue; yelling all over the place, she was, every time her an' Aggie had a few words. Still, Aggie an' me get along all right. Yes, I'll come in in the morning an' give her a hand. Glad to. You ain't finished while you can stir about, I always say. The pension's killed off more old tough 'uns than work ever did.' She laughed heartily at her own wit, and I took advantage of the slackening of the spate to say hastily, 'Nine o'clock, then,' and beat a retreat.

Dahlia arrived next evening, just as the cyclamen and lilac colours were fading from the sky. I heard the dry skid of a hastily braked car and ran down to the gate, realising as I did so that I was not the only one who had been buying things during this month since our return. Dahlia's car was long and white and carried more chromium plate than a milk-bar. The back seats were piled with suit-cases and hat-boxes shrouded in initialled linen; and flung carelessly beside them was a fur coat which even my untrained sense informed me had cost more than all my dogs would do, though they lived each to be twenty and had pups (those that could) every year. She swung her slim legs out of the car and sat there, sideways, smiling at me. 'So I have found it,' she said, and held up her face like a child for a welcoming kiss. I put my head down and sniffed. 'Ah, Jeunesse Dorée again, isn't it? How nice to see you and smell you again, Dahlia.' I walked round the car and got in at the other side. 'I don't know how you'll feel about lodging this shining thing in a barn, but there's no choice. I'll come round with you. The gate is just up here on the left; you'll have to go slowly.'

By the glitter of its coachwork, no more, the car was steered through the old farm gate that led to the barn, and just at the crucial moment when I was straining my neck to see if we had cleared the posts, something seized and pulled my left ear. I turned round and found myself staring into the solemn face of a little monkey. 'Hell,' I said, 'let go my ear! I suppose this abortion is yours?'

'Not exactly my abortion, my monkey,' said Dahlia gravely, breathing carefully as she took the turning into the barn. 'I didn't exactly mean to buy a monkey,' she continued, 'but I bought it from an organ-grinder because it was ill, and, as he had no home he could not look after it properly. It hasn't a very nice nature – yet.'

'But you trust that living with you will improve it.'

Dahlia showed her glorious teeth in a small controlled smile. 'I smack it regularly, now that it's better,' she said hopefully. 'Merciful Father, what is this? They will eat the monkey and me, too.'

All the dogs came streaming round the corner of the house, and ran, barking and sniffing, towards the strange woman who bore something even more strange in her arms. I dispersed them with words, rough or soothing, and a few pushes. Then I said to Dahlia, who was now helpless with laughter, 'Let's run into the house. The boy who does the garden will bring your bags in, if he hasn't gone.'

We ran over the cobbles to the back door, and as I ran and pushed and shouted, cursing myself for not having thought to tie up the dogs, I saw Agnes looking out of the kitchen window. The window was of old glass and the greenish tinge of it made Agnes look like a fish pressing up to the wall of an aquarium; nevertheless, I could see her expression clearly. Interested at first, in this my first visitor, it slowly changed to a kind of incredulous horror. The reason for this change eluded me.

I opened the door that led to the front of the house and let Dahlia through ahead of me, and then, leaning back so that my voice would carry to the kitchen, I shouted, 'Agnes, ask Billy to bring the bags in, they're in the car. Or if he's gone get them in yourself, will you?' I took Dahlia up to her room, which I had filled with her name-flowers in lemon and apricot colours, and I sat on her bed and tried to hold the monkey while she took off her hat and smoothed her hair with her fingers. She had the loveliest head, small and oval and rather pressed in at the temples as though it had been moulded carefully between a craftsman's hands, and her hair clung to it, black and silky and smooth, except over the eyes where a few tiny flat C-shaped curls fell over her forehead.

'You are thin,' I said, watching her; 'thinner than ever. I'm going to stuff you up with soup and milk and things. How long can you stay?'

'Oh, a long time,' she said vaguely. 'I'm sick of London, anyway, and November is coming. If I like it here I think

I'll "build a willow cabin at your gate". Would you mind?'

'Mind, I should love it. But why build? There's plenty of room here and you're welcome for ever.'

'I wish everybody was as nice as you.'

'Everybody doesn't owe you what I do.'

Dahlia gave me a brief smile that hadn't much heart in it. 'Show me the garden while it's still light enough,' she said.

'There's not much to see now, but wait till next year. What are you going to do with that?' I asked, nodding towards the monkey.

'I'll slip its chain under the leg of the bed,' said Dahlia, doing so as she spoke. 'It's a good little thing, really. It'll lie on the bed quite quietly. Poor scrap. Why are they so pathetic, Polly? Is it because they're so like us. Look at its nails.'

She lifted the tiny paw and I looked at it. The nails were really rather amazing.

It clung to her hand for a moment, uttering little squeaky noises, and then settled itself with an oddly resigned gesture on the end of the eiderdown.

We went down and walked slowly round the darkening garden that was full of the cool earthy scent of raked soil and chrysanthemums. The mist was gathering so quickly that before we had completed the circuit the smoke from our cigarettes was lost in it.

Indoors again I held a match to the fire, and the fact that the flames leaped up bravely and bit into the sticks with a crackle seemed to fit the enchantment of the evening, and the company, and the pleasant feeling that had shot through me when I had said, at the sight of the gathering mist, 'It'll be another nice day tomorrow.' It was grand to think that tomorrow would find me here, and Dahlia here, and everything just the same.

Dahlia went upstairs to put on one of the trailing dresses of which she was so fond. Almost at once she was on the stairs, calling in the husky whisper that served her for a shout, 'Polly, my things haven't been brought up.'

'All right,' I called back. 'I'll see about them. That boy is a fool.'

I went into the kitchen, from which came sounds of animated conversation. Tommy sat by the glowing range eating his supper of bread and dripping. Mrs Pawsey was pinning on her ancient hat and talking over her shoulder to Agnes and a woman whom, from her resemblance to Agnes, I judged to be the redoubtable Cissie. The conversation stopped at my entry. Mrs Pawsey drove home the last of the fierce pins which secured the erection to her top-knot, and with a spatter of 'good nights' made her way to the door and was gone.

'Cissie dropped in for a bit of a chat,' said Agnes shortly.

Surprising, perhaps, but not unlikely. Rows between the members of such families spring up very suddenly and die down just as quickly.

'Did you tell Billy about the bags?' I began.

'He'd gone,' said Agnes.

'Then why didn't you get them in? I asked you to,' I said, speaking more abruptly than was my wont because of the look of sharp interest upon Cissie's face.

Agnes put her hands on her hips.

'I have fell low,' she said, speaking slowly and with dignity. 'I have fell low, but I have not fell so low as that. I'm not going to wait on no nigger.'

The import and the insolence of the words staggered me for a second. Then I said, 'Blast you! How dare you speak to me like that?'

'I didn't use language, anyway,' said Agnes.

'Wouldn't soil her tongue,' added Cissie.

God, I was so furious that I thought I would choke.

'Get out of this kitchen,' I said in a low, strangled voice. 'Get out, now, both of you.' I should have loved to have added Cissie's farewell, 'And take your bastard with you,' but the child in question was sitting there, bread and dripping poised, mouth and eyes wide, drinking in the drama of yet another row.

45

'Glad to,' said Agnes. 'And, before I go, let me tell you, Miss Phyllis, that if your mother could see you now, using such language and keeping such company, she'd turn in her grave, poor dear lady, that she would.'

'Good for you, Ag,' said Cissie.

I was helpless. Furious words certainly formed themselves in my mind, agonising for utterance – but what could the most searing words do against such ignorant, barbarous self-righteousness? What they both wanted was a bloody good smack of the head, and they came damn near getting it, too. 'Get your things and be quick,' I said to the chief offender, 'and you take Tommy and wait outside.'

With elaborate insolence Cissie straightened Tommy's hair, pulled his coat straight, and moved slowly with him to the door. I pushed it to after her smartly enough to catch her a bump on her heel and her fat behind.

I stood in the kitchen, listening to Agnes blundering about overhead, until the direction of the noise changed and she came clumping down the stairs with the wicker dress-basket under her arm. She paused at the foot of the back stairs.

'Well, what are you waiting for?'

'My money.'

I laughed. That did touch her a little. I saw the aloof, righteously-injured expression break up to admit a glimpse of annoyance. So I went on laughing, long after I could have stopped.

'Don't be funny,' I said, at last, still smiling. 'You don't get any money. I'm not sure that I shan't sue you for leaving without notice.'

'You told me to go.'

'Because you defied me and insulted my guest. Now are you going to walk out, or have I got to throw you?'

Agnes made for the door.

Shaking, and struggling against tears of impotent fury, I went out to Dahlia's car and fetched in the luggage. How I wished, weakly, that I had done it myself in the first place and so never set match to the piled tinder of Agnes's strange

46

hatred. But even so, I reflected, she would have struck over something else she was asked to do for Dahlia: and it was far better that she should be gone now, before she had had time or chance to insult Dahlia to her face and so hurt her.

Would any one have believed it? Nineteen thirty-seven, in enlightened England, within seventy miles of the city that is the heart of a multicoloured Empire – 'I'm not going to wait on no nigger'. Dahlia, clever, cultured, the loveliest thing that Agnes's little pig eyes had ever rested on, to be dismissed with that one scornful, ignorant word.

God, I was angry. So angry that the inside of my head felt hot and raw. And when, dumping down the last bag in Dahlia's room I caught sight of my own face in the glass, I was glad that on my way upstairs I had prepared a good lie to account for my discomposure.

'My woman's brat has come out full of rash,' I said as casually as I could. 'It may not be anything, but she thought she'd rather not stay here, and I didn't want her to.'

'How awful,' said Dahlia. 'Has she got anywhere to go?'

'Her home's in the village,' I said shortly. 'There you are. Now I expect you to prepare for me a perfect vision of beauty, because the boy had gone and I've lost a lot of sweat getting them up.'

Not, I thought to myself, that Dahlia would look better in any clothes ever designed than she did at that moment, naked except for a narrow brassiere and a pair of very brief knickers, with every muscle and, it seemed, every bone, visibly and exquisitely sculptured under that warm coffee-coloured skin. I could have yelled with rage over a state of society in which Agnes, large and raw and surly and stupid, could, by virtue of her completely English hide, take up so superior an attitude.

I went down into the deserted kitchen and lifted the lids of the saucepans that were simmering on the stove. Except for boiling eggs and milk on the smelly gas-rings of odious bed-sittingrooms, I hadn't looked into a saucepan since I had done so, long ago, in this very kitchen, when I used to peep to see how the Christmas puddings were doing, or scooped out a spoonful of green peas, which I much preferred uncooked – and still do.

I identified the bread sauce with a clove-stuck onion like a medieval plague-ball riding in the middle, and the potatoes, the cauliflower and the gravy. Then I opened the oven door and, blinking in the wave of hot air that rushed to meet me, surveyed the chicken and some kind of pudding in a glass pie dish. Baste, I thought, one bastes chickens. I endeavoured to do so, scooping fat from the tin with a kitchen spoon and pouring it over the browning fowl. Then I burnt my hand on the tin and put the whole affair back hastily.

I mixed the dogs' dinner in an enormous bowl and doled it out into separate pans, over which I stood to see that the greedy ones didn't steal from the others. When they had finished I shut them in the kitchen, went into the lounge and poured myself a glass of sherry. Tomorrow, I thought, I must find some one to take Agnes's place: and would Mrs Pawsey turn up, or would sedition have spread? I brooded for a bit over Agnes's reference to Mother. No doubt she was right. The idea of an exotic half-caste who had been on the stage, installed with an organ-grinder's monkey in the best spare bedroom, would be enough to make Mother 'turn in her grave'.

But so, after all, would a great many things that were inseparable from my mode of life. Mother had been dead for twenty years and things had changed. She had lived a sheltered life of the kind that didn't exist any more. She had pleased herself during her chatelaineship and I must do the same.

The fact remained, nagging at me, that Mother could have quelled rebellion in Agnes, or any one else, with a look. If she had invited a Chinese juggling troupe to occupy the house Agnes would have waited on them without a word. I knew that. In some almost occult way Agnes knew that Mother was strongly rooted in depths of respectability and moral rectitude, therefore whatever she did was right. I wasn't, therefore whatever I did was wrong. Probably my unquestioning acceptance of, and attempted kindness to Tommy, 'the bastard', had set Agnes, in some perverse way, against me at the very beginning. To the intolerant tolerance is a most intolerable thing.

Dahlia came down in a dress of silver-grey velvet with the neck gathered like the calyx of a flower and tied with a thick cord of coral-coloured silk. A lovely dress, a tasteful dress, a costly dress, but not the dress for her because, although it emphasised the vividness of her lips, the brightness of her eyes, the almost lacquered brilliance of her hair, it threw up distinctly the duskiness of her powdered skin. Sometimes, in brown or black clothing she might have been Italian or Provençal. Tonight there was no mistaking. A pity. Yet why, after all, deplore the means by which such beauty was attained?

I poured more sherry and sat gloating over the companionship of which I had suddenly felt the need forty-eight hours before.

Presently Dahlia wrinkled her nose, studied the end of her cigarette and then looked round.

'Something is burning,' she said. I sniffed, smelt nothing but burning wood and tobacco for a moment, and then my slower senses became aware of the stealthy, acrid scent.

'Oh, blast Agnes,' I cried, leaping from my chair.

'Why?'

'For having a brat and letting it get spots,' I yelled back and flung myself kitchenwards. Billows of blue smoke were pouring from the oven. The chicken was much browner than it need have been, and the pie dish was full of something very much like coke. I dropped it into the sink and turned the tap.

The rest of the meal was perfect, for the overbrowned skin of the chicken didn't matter, and the flesh had not dried. Dahlia hardly ate any of it. She pushed her food about her plate and pretended, but it was easy to see why she was so thin. I had a sudden, vivid memory of the way in which, on the day of our meeting, we had fallen upon those thick ham sandwiches, munching hungrily, scooping up every crumb.

Dahlia seemed to have outgrown such a simple pleasure, but I was still fond of food. I thought – as I savoured the smoothness of the sauce and crushed the delightful slight brittleness of the cauliflower – that people who are indifferent to food, Penelope for example, miss a great deal of quite harmless and regular pleasure. Love of food, like love of other crude comforts, is a thing that you can take with you along the years and enjoy when you're quite old. You don't have to be clever or pretty or nimble as you have to be for the enjoyment of intellectual, erotic or sporting pleasure. A comfortable chair, a good fire, a hot-water bottle in its season, soft underclothes – we don't give them honour enough. Once, I remember, after the shattering end of a love affair, I went to bed with my hot-water bottle clutched to my chest that felt bursting with the tears I would not shed. I thought, 'I've got a bed, and I'm still alive; I can still appreciate the comfort of heat, this isn't the end of everything'. And I soon slept.

I said now to Dahlia, 'You don't seem to be making much of a meal. Don't you like it?'

'I'm loving it,' she said, untruthfully, and pushed it about some more.

Presently I took away the plates and dishes, and, with apologies for burning the pudding, set a bowl of fruit on the table. Dahlia shook her head at it and took a cigarette. There were nectarines in the dish too, and large William pears with all the richness of autumn in their scent, as well as crunchy red apples.

'Well,' I said, 'if you won't eat we needn't sit here any longer. It's warmer in the lounge. Go across and put some logs on. I'll just make some coffee. It won't take a minute.'

I took a pear with me and ate it, with the juice running over my fingers, while I heated the milk. Then I carried the tray along the passage, pushed the door shut with my heel and drew up the little table to the fire. Dahlia lay back in a chair with the firelight on her face, and for just a moment, until she realised that I was looking at her and smiled at me, I saw and recognised upon her face the same expression of despair that had arrested my attention all that time ago in the tea-shop.

It was gone immediately. I returned her smile, poured the coffee, set her cup within reach, lighted a cigarette and sat down. All the time I was wondering what had happened. Nothing much, probably. Dahlia was very easily depressed and just as easily elated. I'd known her to weep because she was disappointed over a hat that she'd liked better in the shop than she did when she got it home; and, anyway, I'd got her under my roof. I'd be tactful, and yet fuss her a little, feed her up if I could, and listen to any complaints she had with patience. After all, I had saved her, in a way, from despair and poverty; and that gave me almost an omnipotent feeling where she was concerned.

That set me off reflecting upon the mystery of personality. How could any one regard it as a static thing? How could any one ever make definite and final remarks about it? With Dahlia I could be maternal and tolerant, kind, and sensible, a trifle domineering – and yet I am not a tolerant, maternal, kind, sensible or domineering person in other relationships. I roused myself from these unprofitable reflections and picked up my coffee, which immediately went slopping into the saucer as my hand gave a jerk at the sound of a shrill screaming, a growling and pounding that came from the room immediately overhead – Dahlia's room.

'The dogs, that monkey!' I cried, and took the stairs two at a time. They had got it. Block and Velvet and the mongrels united for once in an act of destruction, like the incongruous allies that a war will make anywhere. Agnes, I remembered, had left the door of the back stairs open and they had slunk out of the kitchen and up that way.

The shoes Dahlia had taken off stood near. I took one in either hand and drove them off. It was too late. The monkey was literally torn to pieces and the little red collar and the silver chain that had prevented it from escaping were still swinging, blood-bespattered, from the foot of the bed. Block was still growling and slavering, so I gave him another blow for good measure, and was going, in strict justice, to deal three more for the others, when Dahlia's voice said, 'Don't hit them, hit me'. She was hanging on the door and her face was the colour of dirty ashes. Instinctively I moved so that I stood between her and the remains.

'It's dead,' I said, 'but it died quickly.'

'It's all my fault. I tied it there and then didn't shut the door properly. That monkey was fond of me.'

'I'm most awfully sorry,' I said. And at the sound of my voice speaking soothingly the four dropped tails began to wag, feverishly apologetic.

'Go downstairs, blast you, you horrible brutes,' I cried. I pointed the way, shoe in hand, and they dropped their tails again and trailed out, one behind the other. 'You go down, too, and sit on something, Dahlia, please. I'll clear this away, and bury it decently. I can't tell you how sorry – but do go on down now, and get a drink or something, and don't fling a faint on me into the bargain.'

'I should apologise to you,' said Dahlia with a gulp. I pushed the door on her, and holding back a shuddering nausea with an effort that was only just sufficient I gathered up the bits into a box and scrubbed the carpet. A damn fine beginning to a visit, I thought, as I tugged the bed forward to hide the wet patch. And so exactly like Dahlia, my mind went on while I was washing my hands, to bring a monkey into a houseful of dogs and then not shut the door securely. If it had been the action of any one else in the world I should have said, 'Serve you right', but with Dahlia in it the miserable little drama had the pathos of an orphan child losing its rag doll. I hurried down to her.

'Forget it, if you can,' I said awkwardly, for even with her tenderness is not my *métier*. 'It didn't suffer.'

Dahlia mustered her meaningless smile.

'Poor Polly, don't bother about it any more. You can't expect dogs to be wiser than people who distrust anything that's a trifle different and would destroy it if they could. Let's forget it. But I'm grateful to you for coping with it.'

I looked round the room and then said briskly, 'Do you see that piano? That's been put there specially for you. If you're not too tired you might try it.'

'I'm not tired at all. In fact, I'd rather work than just tinkle. Isn't there something nice and new and a bit hard we could tackle?'

'Well,' I said, with the senseless diffidence that always comes over me when I have to produce some untried stuff, 'I had a bit of an idea for that old woman's song in *Slave's Saga*. A moaning kind of thing, with a good strong beat in it. Like this....'

I gave her my version of my latest creation.

'Got it written? Let's have a look at it.'

I found the words, scribbled on the back of a bill, and gave them to her, together with a good sharp pencil and a sheet or two of lined paper.

'Oh, good title, Polly. "Lawd, Turn Your Face to Me." Just right.' She read out the words in the pseudo-negro pronunciation that had been insisted upon.

'Ah'm singin'
Though Ah'm low as Ah cin be.
Ah'm singin',
Though de Lawd has turned His back on me.
Ah'm waitin' till de sun breaks through,
An' Ah'm singin' cause there's nothin, else to do.

'No sun in Heav'n.
No blue overhead.
Ah'm poor an' Ah'm lonely
An' soon Ah'll be dead.
But Ah'm singin' in the shadows, an' Ah'm singin' in the rain,
Dear Lawd, hear me, turn your face again.

'Ah'm singing'
Though Ah feel that Ah could cry.
Ah'm singing'
Though the days go slippin' by.
Dear Lawd, watch me, brave as Ah cin be.
Hear me singin': turn your face to me.'

'That's splendid, Polly. Just what's wanted, and with that nice bit of variation in the second verse. Mutter it through again. I hope I'll catch it.'

So we began our humming, banging, one-note-striking performance that would have convinced any observer that we were a couple of lunatics, but which did result, at the end of an hour, in a song that was exactly as I had imagined it: a rhythmical thing with a catching tune and with that undernote of patient yearning that would just suit the old woman in *Slave's Saga*.

When Dahlia had finished making squiggly marks, and tucked the pencil, as usual, behind her ear and then played it through, singing in what remained of her voice, I knew it was good. I wasn't conscious, as I had been, of the foolishness of the words or the wealth of repetition. Once again I wanted to hug Dahlia. I knew just how fathers feel towards the mothers of their children, who have taken something shapeless, and in itself useless, and transformed it into something real and living.

I reached out and took hold of one of her thin little hands. It was cold as a leaf.

'You're a marvel,' I said. 'Come over to the fire now and get warm.' But the hand slipped through mine.

'Just a minute. Playing like that has made me want to.' She fingered the notes uncertainly for a moment, and then broke into the song that she knew was one of my favourites, 'The Lute Player'. I sat there by the fire with my arms round my knees, while against the background that was an odd mixture of pictures of Carcassonne and fairy-tale illustrations I watched the story unfold for the hundredth time.

> 'There was a lady, great and splendid,
> I was a minstrel in her halls . . .'

She brought out the strong chord at 'immortal', and then whispered the end, 'immortal, by virtue of my hate – and love'. I said, 'Thank you. You know you can still sing, Dahlia.'

'At a range of six yards; no more.'

'And now that I've heard it once again, perfectly, I never want to hear it again. Will you remember that?' I told her about my other records.

'I suppose,' said Dahlia, eyeing me with her head on one side, 'that you have a private life that none of us know anything about?'

'Everyone has,' I said.

'Listen to this. See what you think of it. I made it all myself after the style of those little tinkling songs – Elizabethan, aren't they?'

She fingered the notes again, and then, very softly, and it seemed, inconsequently, voice and notes ran together.

> 'My body goes a-whoring
> After strange men
> Who hold her and ravish her and leave her and then
> My soul goes in search and brings her home again.
>
> 'My body, like a greedy sheep
> Must go astray
> In the strange fields and the new pastures all through the day
> But my soul always chides her home your way.
>
> 'The strange men are forgotten,
> The new spells fade.
> And after all the mouths have met and the hunger's allayed
> My soul like a sheep-dog chases home the jade.'

The little tinkling notes, so light that it might have been the virginal beneath her fingers, fainted on the air. I was silent for a moment, then I said,

'Hell, if you made that all yourself you'll soon be able to

do without me. I'm very jealous.'

'You needn't be. You see, I borrowed most of the words. And, anyway, it's *verboten* to mention the soul, these days.'

'Well, come over here then, and have a drink and cherish the body for a bit.'

'In half a minute.' She played a short tune through twice and then, just strumming softly, threw her voice at me over the sound. 'Polly, tell me, how black am I?'

My heart, that usually well-controlled organ, gave a leap, as if I had been faced suddenly with a dreadful, personal danger. My breath went, and even if I had had an answer ready I couldn't have spoken for a moment. But my mind, so far as an answer was concerned, was a blank. Colour was a thing that had never been mentioned between us . . . and I realised then, for the first time, that we had accorded it the silence that one accords an affliction, fits, a clubfoot, a harelip. What could one say? It was like being faced by an insane person asking, 'How mad am I?'

Crazy answers formed themselves. 'Why ask me?' 'You should know.' I couldn't say that kind of thing, of course. I couldn't say anything.

At last I forced myself to look at her. Her eyes were fixed on my face. It was as though her soul were drowning and clinging by means of her eyes to me, sole hope of safety. A silly simile. Souls don't drown and eyes can't cling. But it felt like that. There was nothing about her but those searching eyes, and the fingers that went on drawing sound from a box of wood and wire. I quibbled.

'I don't quite get your meaning,' I said slowly. 'You aren't *black at all*.'

'How white am I, then?'

'Very white.' I said foolishly. 'More than half . . .'

'When you first saw me, Polly, that day at the table, did you know at once?'

'Know what?' I asked, fighting for time.

'That I wasn't white.' Her voice was relentless. I gave up the struggle.

'Dahlia,' I said, 'I don't know whether you appreciate what hellish awkward questions you're asking me; but I suppose you want an answer and I suppose you want the truth. Yes, I did.'

Ought I to have said that? If it wasn't plain from her mirror, and Heaven knew she looked in it enough, ought I to have told her? Why not? It was the truth, and though I frequently lie in the way of business, and occasionally in my personal dealings, I avoid it when possible if the matter seems important, or if I like the person to whom I am talking. But even when I had taken that fence I wasn't safely on the level. Dahlia was working towards something, of what I had no idea. She said, quite calmly, 'Of course, I knew that really. It sticks out a mile. And even if the Haiti miracle worked for me there'd still be my hands, my feet, something in the way I walk. Wouldn't there?'

I nodded, and then partly to sidetrack the issue and partly from curiosity, I said, 'The Haiti miracle. What's that? And do for the love of God stop that fiddling. You're getting on my nerves.'

'Sorry,' she said, and got up and, coming over to the hearth, threw herself down in one smooth movement so that she was sitting at my feet and the faint perfume of the Jeunesse Dorée rose to meet me.

'They say,' she began, 'that in Haiti there grows a seed that will turn even a full-blooded negro white, if it doesn't kill him. Some slaves discovered it, many years ago, and some died, but those that didn't were made white. So many tried after that, as the legend grew and strengthened, and so many died of it, that the white men went about destroying the plant that grew it. But it is still found in places and it's still believed in. You'd have to be very brave to try it, I suppose.'

She broke off and looked into the fire, and I hoped that the discussion would end there.

'But, Polly, does it matter?'

'Does what matter?'

'Colour.'

'In what way? And to whom?'

'To you, for instance.'

'Not a scrap . . . if you mean do I mind it. Actually, it gives you something, I think, a decorative quality, and, quite possibly, a talent that you wouldn't otherwise have.'

I was conscious a trifle too late of the shallow selfishness of that speech. It was as though I had said, 'I don't mind your being off-white so long as you're good to look at and have a talent that can serve me.' So I added an amendment, quite genuine, too. And in a sense it was an insurance against anything more that she might ask.

'Besides that, Dahlia, I like *you*. If you suddenly lost your looks and went stone deaf, you'd still be there, with all the things that make you *you*. Do you see? So what colour you are can't matter.'

'It matters to some people,' said Dahlia heavily. 'You're an exceptional person, Polly . . . and you're a girl.'

I knew then that we had reached the heart of the problem. I knew then that Dahlia was in love with somebody who was white, and who minded her not being.

'Have a drink,' I said. Dahlia nodded. I went across to the built-in cupboard in the white-panelled wall, against which the tall branches of Michaelmas daisies cast slender shadows that danced in the leaping firelight. It used to be called 'the jam cupboard,' I remembered, and I used to stand there in the days of my greedy childhood gloating over the shapes of the whole strawberries pressing against the jars. I took out the whisky and the siphon and the glasses, and thought as I poured hers that I'd make it strong. Then if she wanted to tell me it'd help her, and if she wanted to forget it, it'd help her do that, too. As for me, I needed a drink darn badly.

I suppose I might have guessed that this was what would happen to Dahlia, sooner or later; but now that it had happened I was taken aback. Heaps of people suffer from unrequited love, it's as common a trouble as a cold in the head, and as unpleasant to watch. But those people can mostly snap out of it and look elsewhere, and usually do. But Dahlia's problem wasn't quite so simple. After all, if people with cross-eyes could only marry cross-eyed people, you'd be a little sorry for them, wouldn't you? And it seemed to me that Dahlia's field was more constricted than cross-eyes could make it. She ought to fall in love with somebody just as much white and just as much black as she was. And where would you find him?

She stretched up her hand for the glass and I caught a sight of her face as she turned. I thought, she wants to tell me about it, that's why she's looking at me like that – a dog wanting a bone and not daring to ask.

I said, as gently as I could, feeling horribly self-conscious, 'Would you like to tell me about it? Who is it?'

'Roger Hayward,' she said, with a promptitude that justified my question.

I lifted my glass, just to give me a moment in which I need neither speak nor look at her. But it was no good. The glass banged against my teeth and a thin stream of liquid dribbled out of the corner of my mouth and began to run over my chin. I caught it with a flick of my tongue and swallowed before I said, 'Poor Dahlia.'

'Poor bloody fool?'

'Yes, poor bloody fool.'

'Two nights ago,' said Dahlia, thoughtfully, 'he said the cruellest thing to me.'

'I believe you. He has a gift for it.'

'Do you know him well?'

'Pretty well. And you?'

'I've slept with him,' said Dahlia simply.

That time I managed a good long drink.

'Go on, tell me about it if you want to.'

So I sat there and listened to the story, the oldest story; the story that Eve's daughters – if she had any – got together and told in the evenings, the story that Eve – if she overheard it – would recognise as the curse beginning to work out. They'd met at a party, Maisie's or somebody's.

'He sort of hung around and looked at me,' said Dahlia, and my heart skipped another beat, remembering, as it did, that look.

'There's something,' said Dahlia, to the fire, 'about that look. It's like a compliment, or a bouquet, or a sonnet being laid at your feet by an Elizabethan courtier. It transports you, translates, just a look. You know?'

I nodded. I knew.

'It began there. I can't tell you how it went on. We danced. He said the most impossibly flattering things – things that you might read, or perhaps imagine, but never expect to hear spoken, and all in that matter-of-fact voice of his, as though he were talking about the weather. I hadn't any will left, or any sense. There was nothing left but my body and that was gaining a consciousness of itself that it had never had before.'

'I know,' I said. 'That's the effect of the tremendous animal magnetism, vitality, sex-appeal, call it what you like, which is the *only* thing, the absolutely *only* thing that he has in any unusual quantity.'

Dahlia twisted round and looked up at me.

'You know a lot about him, don't you, Polly?'

'Yes,' I parried, 'I know a lot about him.' More than you, probably, I thought; I'm more critical. 'Go on.'

'There isn't much to tell – especially since you understand. It just went on. He came to the flat and stayed sometimes. I was mad, of course, to get into such a tangle of feeling. To let it be heaven when he was there and hell other times. We didn't go out much – only to meals at quiet places, or in the car, or to places like Maisie's. Two nights ago I just happened to suggest going some place to dance – Greegi's, and he said . . . ' I waited through the pause, knowing what was coming. 'And he said, "My dear Dahlia, I know a great many people in London; some of them rich, many of them useful, if somewhat reactionary in their views. I can't afford to be seen in a place like Greegi's with a

60

coloured song writer." I,' Dahlia added unnecessarily, 'am the coloured song writer.'

'What did you do?'

'I laughed. God be praised, I laughed and I laughed. It was the sheerest hysteria, but he didn't know that. I said, "Frank must be your middle name." Then he laughed and said, "I'll take you to Marc's." I said, "You'll take me to hell!" And he didn't know how true that was either. Then we had some drinks and he wanted to stay the night. But I proffered the unsurmountable and he went away. In the morning he rang up, but I put on a voice and said that Miss Whitman had gone out of town and had let the flat. Then your letter came. So here I am. Miserable as the devil, no kind of a guest, Polly.'

'You'll do,' I said. 'And you'll get over it. One does, you know.'

'But it's so unfair. Just this miserable colour, which I can't help. And which doesn't make any difference. I'm not savage or anything like that. Of course, I might have quite black babies.'

'Might you, really?'

'So I have heard. It's a law of nature or something. But I don't see why a possible some one who isn't born should be considered before a person who is already here. Do you?'

'Well, put like that it sounds silly,' I admitted, but there was a grain of doubt in my mind, and my voice must have shown it, for Dahlia said in a voice like a pounce,

'Tell me honestly . . . suppose you really liked a man as much coloured as I am, would you marry him?'

I fended off that question.

'Marry? Did you expect to marry Roger Hayward?'

'Nothing less would be of any use to me.'

'Heaven send you sense. Roger couldn't marry you if you were the Lily Maid of Astolat. He's got a wife in Paris. He goes back to her with astounding regularity after each of his major affairs. He's probably with her now – I hand you that as a compliment.'

Dahlia had scrambled to her feet and stood breathing like an overdriven horse.

'Is that true? Oh, Polly, how did you know? Tell me, tell me everything else you know. Polly, please . . . '

I was fumbling about in my harassed mind to know what to say without betraying myself – for I hadn't yet made up my mind how much I would tell her (if I'd been sure it would help I'd have spilled the whole story, gladly; but I wasn't), and while I was still hesitating Dahlia raised her head in a way that made one think of a deer in some fabulous forest, and said, 'There's some one outside'. At the same time I heard Velvet's fussy bark from the kitchen, followed instantly by Block's more menacing note.

Agnes come back, full of apologies, I thought. So I closed the door carefully behind me lest some incautious word should reach Dahlia. I opened the door and saw some little lights shining. I switched on the globe over the porch and waited on the step while a decrepit little Austin sighed itself to a standstill and the battered doors of it opened and two figures unfolded themselves on to the gravel. Penelope and Megan, my sisters.

IV

ON how many Friday evenings had I rushed out like this to meet them after a long fidgety wait at the window with my nose pressed white and flat to the cold pane? From Monday morning to Friday evening they lodged in Stoney in order to be near their school. Father drove them in on Monday – and it was typical of Father that though Pen harnessed the pony and brought the trap round while Megan raided the pantry for tuck and Mother fetched

Father's boots and muffler and pressed the grocer's list into his hand, there was always at least fifteen minutes of impatience and quietly blasphemous waiting before they could set off. 'How I wish,' Pen would mutter, twisting the reins in her hands, 'that Flip could come home by himself. Then Father needn't come. Every Monday of our lives we're late.'

'I miss some beastly algebra,' Megan would say gloatingly. And then, after a careful glance around to see whether Mother had yet emerged from the house, she would unwrap and display some unusual spoil that the raid had afforded.

'You'll never get it there: it's coming through the paper already,' Pen would say. Then Megan would laugh again and say, 'Don't be so superior. You'll be glad enough to eat it, paper and all, after you've seen what Mother Craske has been hatching up for you this week-end.'

I used to hang about and listen and envy them. Their life at Stoney, bounded by the school and Mrs Craske's lodgings, had for me the charm of the unknown. When, years after I explored and knew it, it was very dull. Pen and Megan had left it, of course; the teachers whom I knew by report were gone; and Mrs Craske's were just the first of my dreary lodgings. Also, the war was on and no pantry was worth raiding, even if I had bothered to try.

At last Father would come out, grumbling about being late. He would offer to take the reins; Pen would refuse to relinquish her one hope of speeding up the belated journey; with some relief Father would sink back and with waves and back-called good-byes the girls would go out of my life until Friday evening when the carrier brought them home in company with crates of ducks and hens, netted pigs, or a roped calf.

In summer I met the wagonette on the Green and very proudly carried Pen's satchel of books home for her. In the dark evenings I was far too frightened of the empty road to venture out, even if Mother had allowed it. As a child I was nervous, and there was always a certain relief in the pleasure with which I greeted them on winter Fridays. For three nights the long passages and the big shadowy bedroom held no terrors for me. Penelope had courage, she would face any dark silence. She always went first on our trips to the attic for apples and walnuts. Megan, though more given to carrying candles, was not so nervous as I, and her cheerful loud voice and way of banging doors were as comforting to me as Pen's quieter confidence.

They would come in, blinking at the light, red-nosed and cold-fingered from the slow chilly journey. We always waited tea on Fridays and sat down together to a meal that was neither tea nor supper – stacks of hot toast, a pie of some kind, cheese cakes, and sodden brown farm-house cake, rich with eggs and butter. The week's news was exchanged. 'Pen had top marks in her form again,' Megan would say with generous pride.

Father would say, 'Good girl,' and Mother, 'Mind you keep it up.'

Nobody made any inquiry or volunteered any statement about the progress of Megan's studies, but there were often other things to report. Whispered conversations took place on the stairs or in the hall.

'Would now be a good time, do you think?'

'I think so. They're both in a good mood.'

'Support me, Pen.' Pleading, irresistible voice – almost weeping and yet almost as ready to burst into laughter over the whole ridiculous affair.

'With my life, fool. Come on.'

A strained sort of entry, and then Pen saying in an apologetic way, a trifle casual, none the less:

'Oh, Mother, Mrs Craske sent you a note.' Good, stiff note-paper, supporting Mrs Craske's reputation as a distressed gentlewoman, written all over at odd angles so that Mother, legitimately angry, could turn the pages about with a sharp thwacking noise. It was always a note of complaint, and with one exception, always about Megan. She had complained about her food and refused to eat it. She had left the light burning all night in the corridor after visiting another room – in itself an offence. She had leaned from her bedroom window and talked to some boys. She had consumed some contraband provisions of a sticky nature in her bed and smeared the counterpane. There was no end to her sins. Mother, true to her Victorian upbringing, would pass the letter across to Father, who, putting down his book or paper unwillingly, would say mildly, 'I'm sorry to hear this, Meg.' Mother never said she was sorry. She took care that the sorrow should be Megan's – and incidentally Penelope's and mine. 'There will be no new hats for the summer now. Why should I strain every nerve to provide things for people who have no idea of good manners? You will kindly refrain, both of you, from taking anything out of the pantry, since you make gluttons of yourselves *in bed*. Of all places to eat!' Worst threat of all. 'I shall simply give up all idea of trying to have you properly educated. Learning is wasted upon young hussies whose one idea is to converse with errand boys.'

Pen never made any attempt to dissociate herself from the real criminal. Megan was always very repentant, tearful, profuse in apologies, excuses, good resolutions; and then, finally, smiling through her tears, she would produce some ridiculous aspect of her crime, or of Mrs Craske's fury and offer it for Mother's unsympathetic inspection. Penelope would say, elaborately casual, 'I think Mrs Craske has exaggerated a little, Mother.' Father would smile. I would laugh. And though Mother would retain her hurt and aggrieved aspect all over the week-end, when Monday came and the girls were ready and Megan came up uncertainly, wondering whether she would be kissed or not, Mother always unbent at the last minute and would kiss her and bid her try to be a better girl. And none of the threats really became realities.

If Megan's resolves – or her luck – had held, Fridays were delightful. Warm and comfortable, with the long hours of the week-end (and how long they seemed then!) stretching peacefully ahead, we would troop off to bed, where we ate apples and talked. Megan would imitate Mrs Craske, the staff at the school, and sometimes even Mother, for our entertainment. I would lie longing for the day when I, too, should move and have my being in that strange, exciting world. I think their stories wove the spell for me that other children find in books about impossible schools. I can only remember one complaint that came home about Pen. She had, Mrs Craske wrote, been most dreadfully insulting and offensive at the breakfast table.

'Well, Penelope, if it has come to this! If I can't trust *you*! What happened? And I want the truth, mind.' Mother always said that, though to me both Pen and Megan seemed paragons of honesty. I should have thrown the notes in fragments over the hedge.

'I simply said, "If this is coffee, bring me tea, and if it is tea, bring me coffee." That's all. One day, before I leave, I will insult the old faggot properly, so that she knows what an insult is.'

Father laughed. Mother looked puzzled. 'It's a quotation, Mother,' said Pen kindly.

'But which *was* it?' Mother asked, shocked. 'Couldn't you tell?'

'You never can,' said Megan eagerly; 'she uses the same urn for both.'

'Then *I* shall write Mrs. Craske a note,' said Mother firmly. And did. After that Mrs Craske's complaints lost a little of their power to disturb. Mother's faith was shaken. She did add, however, 'Penelope, I don't care for the word "faggot" used in that connection. You don't have an expensive education in order to pick up slang.'

How long ago! And here was I running down the selfsame steps to meet them with the old excitement, mocking the twenty years or more between.

'Hullo,' I cried. 'Hullo. How lovely of you to come! How

marvellous to see you! Both together, too. Oh, joy!'

'God, I'm stiff!' said Pen, stretching her arms wide with a cracking of elbows and wrists and shoulders.

'And I haven't an unbroken bone,' said Meg; 'two hundred mortal miles! Hullo, Polly, you dear thing. Let's have a look at you. And at the house. Just the same, both of you – or should I say improved? Oh, I am glad to see you. Do you mind us coming like this, all unannounced?'

'You said you had plenty of room, didn't you?' Pen paused in her dragging of bags from the dark interior of the little car. 'Or perhaps you've got the house full of people. We hadn't thought of that, Meg.'

'All the better, a crowd is a treat to me. Come on, I can't wait to get inside. I *made* Pen come; I simply *made* her. I couldn't bear to stay away another minute once I knew. Oh, Polly, what an improvement that white paper is. I say, do you remember that squiggly stuff with the face shapes on it, and how we filled them in with eyes and mouths all the way down the stairs? And wasn't Mother mad?'

Laughing and talking all at once, we arrived at the door of the lounge, which had been the chief living-room in the old days, and it suddenly seemed that the old oil lamp with the red-fringed shade should be standing in the middle of the white-clothed, heavily laden table. Father should be laying aside his book and his crooked glasses, and Mother folding away some piece of mending. Dahlia in her silvery frock, looking up with wide startled eyes, was, for a moment, a figure from a dream.

'These are my sisters. They've come after all,' I said. 'This is Penelope, and this is Megan.' I turned to them. 'This is Dahlia. I've told you all about her, haven't I? Now throw your things down anywhere and get near the fire. Are you hungry? What time did you start?'

I bustled round, turning on more lights and throwing logs on the fire, pouring drinks and fetching the chicken that wasn't yet quite cold. It wasn't until they had both eaten and I had taken away the trays that a kind of exhausted peace settled upon us and I could really look at them. We sat quietly for a little time; the air grew blue with smoke, and I looked at them.

Pen I had seen about two years before, but it was twice that time since I had seen Megan. Pen hadn't altered. Once only and that was after her accident when I first saw her scars, had I seen any difference in her appearance. The long pale plaits that had swung against her thin, childish back and whipped as she turned, were still there, a pale brown, almost unfadeable, colour. They were still neat, but bundled up rather ungracefully at the back of her head, exactly as they had been when she first put her hair 'up'. She herself had always been pale and thin, and there had always been frown lines between her eyes and beneath them where she screwed them when she read or looked at anything attentively. They had deepened a little, that was all. Her face couldn't sag or fall into folds because there was only the bony structure of it covered with skin that looked dry and rather hard. There was something slightly mummified about it, except when she was speaking or smiling. She had one supremely good feature, blue eyes, set deeply and fringed with up-curled lashes many shades darker than her hair. They might have been envied by many a woman more beautiful, and her brows had been nice, too; thin and mobile and dark; but one of the scars began just in the middle of her left eyebrow, dividing it in halves with a little bare patch and drawing it up. That gave her face a slightly supercilious expression which made people shy with her and even fear her a little. The other scar ran from just above her lip, through the hollow of her cheek to her ear. Both scars were on the same side, so that there was one profile untouched; and for several times after the accident when I saw her I used to take pains to sit or walk on her unblemished side. But after a time I got used to them; and they weren't in the least horrible, just dry-looking white seams, like pieces of cord.

Looking from Pen with satisfaction, I gazed at Megan with surprise. Remembering, as I did, her letter, I was prepared for change, a fading, a coarsening, a threat, if no more, of what havoc the years could work. But any change there was seemed for the better. Her hair might be hennaed, but it was bright and 'live'-looking, and more attractively arranged than I had ever seen it – but then I thought that almost every time I saw her. It was cut short and curled over the middle of her forehead in a style reminiscent of the old pompadour, and after that it went back sleekly over her crown until it broke into another cluster of curls at the nape of her neck. Under the reddish gold of it her thin pencilled eyebrows showed the darker and her eyes, paler than Pen's, in fact, appeared to have the same deep glow. A vivid lipstick emphasised the curves of her mouth that hadn't sagged or pursed or dropped into that vague expression of discontent that is seen on so many faces in the middle years. Megan was still 'our pretty sister'.

Why had she written me that eagerly miserable letter about the lost joys of being thirty? I threw out a feeler.

'And how is Henry?' Her eyes softened.

'He's very well. Busy, you know, but blooming.'

Curiosity nibbled at me. Why had she come home alone, a thing she had never done before? On one of their holidays I had heard her say, laughingly to some one, 'Outposts of Empire aren't safe for grass widowers.' And once she had insisted upon going back with him just after a sharp attack of 'flu when she really shouldn't have travelled.

Dahlia sat brooding over the fire while we three indulged in reconstructive and reminiscent chatter, until Pen said, 'I'd like to hear some of these wonderful songs'; then she got up like an obedient child and sat down at the piano again. I took advantage of the move to slip away and go upstairs to get out sheets and blankets. The dogs, glad to be liberated from disgraced exile in the kitchen, pattered after me. I went out to the dark garden and gathered blindly a handful of dew-wetted Michaelmas daisies. And that reminded me of Pen's Austin. I got into it to drive it under the cover of the cart-shed. It seemed very small and the miniature wheel and the frail willingness of the little engine were rather pathetic. Pen, I thought had been doing important work of the kind people call 'good', for many years; Dahlia and I had merely enlivened a few of folks' leisure moments; but the barn held Dahlia's glittering toy-bright affair and my heavy roadster, while this little drudge chuffed itself into the cart-shed. There seemed a slight discrepancy in the awards, I felt.

Back in the house I took a childish pleasure in arranging the flowers and in slipping hot-water bottles between the new sheets, warm from the airing cupboard. And I thought about the next day, what we would do, how I would feed them, how Pen should rest and Megan sort out her troubles, whatever they were, in the peace and quiet of Pedlar's Green. As I passed Dahlia's door I thought about her and Roger Hayward. Perhaps I might even help her, too. I could at least point out to her the ruthless, hard, but effective path of reasoning that had led me out of the slough of infatuation to the upland of acceptance where I now, emotionally, dwelt.

Oh, I was full of plans and hope and confidence, bred, no doubt, of the fact that it was my house, that I had gathered the three of them into the shelter of my roof. Their physical well-being depended, for the moment, upon me. And that led me to think, with an arrogance like the arrogance of parenthood, that I could deal with their spiritual states as well.

I went down to offer night-caps, anything from whisky and soda to Ovaltine. It had been the most satisfactory evening of my life.

Remembering Agnes's departure, and the fact that Mrs Pawsey never arrived until after nine, I had set my alarm-clock for six. It was still darkish when its twanging woke me. Block and Velvet who slept in my room, stirred and stretched, looking at me inquiringly through half-closed eyes. I put on my dressing-gown and slippers, ran a comb through my hair, and went down into the silent, sleeping house. The puppies got up from their mat in the hall and I opened the door so that the four dogs could go into the garden and not impede me. Stoves first. The boiler fire was still faintly aglow, so I fed it with sticks and laid on a few handfuls of coke, and breathed sighs of relief when it seemed not to resent the lack of thorough cleaning. The dining-room fire I lit as soon as I had cleaned the grate, and it went out twice. That soured my temper and made me think gloomily of the washing up that I must do before breakfast, for though I had plenty of crockery my supply of plates and knives was limited.

However, when at last the sticks were crackling, and I went into the kitchen, which faced east, the sun was rising, throwing a pinkish light on the whitewashed walls, and I felt better. I let the tap over the sink run until the water steamed, and then I plunged into the washing up with a will. I congratulated myself upon installing the hot-water system and thought with a kind of horror of the methods that had been in force in this very kitchen during my youth. I had a vision of the numerous chilled, chapped chilblained hands that had set great black kettles on the smoky fire of that Moloch of a range, which I could now ignore. Yet not one of the chilblained ones had ever, I was sure, walked out on Mother, or her predecessors, as Agnes had walked out on me.

Time before eight o'clock partakes, I discovered, of the slippery quality of the night hours. By the time that I had swept the most obvious dust off the flat surfaces in the dining-room and set the table and cut the rind off the bacon, it was full morning, the sun was shining brilliantly, and it was time for morning tea. I switched on the kettle and ran upstairs to make myself tidy.

I took Dahlia's tea first. She was awake, sitting up in the bed with a book in one hand and a cigarette in the other. She eyed me with startled guilt. 'I forgot about your woman. I could have helped you; I've been awake ages,' she said.

'Haven't you slept well?' I asked, with proper hostess concern, and something more. Dahlia detected the something.

'I always wake early in a strange bed,' she said. 'I'll just drink this, then I'll come and help you.'

'At your peril,' I said. 'I've done all the work and I want all the credit.'

I went on to the big room that I had once shared with Pen and Megan. I put the tray on the chest between the two beds and poured out three cups of tea. Pen sprang up, awake at once, and took hers, but Megan turned over and mumbled and moaned a bit. I sat on the foot of Pen's bed to drink my tea and gloat anew over the knowledge that here we were together again. I had not realised that the clan feeling could be so strong in me.

Suddenly, and for the first time, I missed the noise of hens cackling and cows lowing as they moved to pasture after the milking, and of jingling harness from the outgoing teams that had been the aural background of our childhood.

'Do you remember,' I began on impulse with the almost threadbare phrase, 'that red-headed boy called Alf Wicker who used to do the sticks and things?'

Megan hitched herself up in the bed and reaching for her tea said, 'I should think I do. He was the first boy I ever kissed.'

'You didn't,' I said, recalling the red-scrubbed face and the gappy teeth and the manury smell that were indistinguishable from the memory that 'Alf' called up.

'I did too. It was behind a haystack. I had the most awful yen for him. I must have been a most disgustingly amorous child.'

There was a kind of caressing regret in her voice.

'I'm glad Mother didn't catch you,' said Pen.

'So'm I,' said Megan over the edge of her cup.

This morning, I noticed, she looked much older than

Pen. Sleep had blurred the features of her face, whose chief charm lay in its delicacy; her skin looked sallow too and her hair was all flat and eclipsed under a net. Pen's pale plaits, slightly ruffled and falling over her shoulders, gave her an oddly childish look.

Standing about the room and casting prismatic colours on the white walls and ceiling were the cut-glass bottles and jars that made up the greater part of Megan's luggage. Skin foods and cleansing creams and astringent lotions and eye-washes. I had inspected them all in other bedrooms where I had visited her; and I had often wondered when, if ever, I should have time and money to invest in a similar display, and what, exactly, the result would be if I did.

I looked now from the bottles to Megan's face and was reminded of a soldier who, laying aside uniform and weapons, reveals himself defenceless. They rise and arm themselves again, the soldier and the beauty, but he may rise to possible victory; she faces certain defeat. For a moment I was sad and the stray sad sentences that wander homeless through time, sensing a harbour in my mind, crowded around. 'A lady whom Time hath surprised.' 'Dust hath filled Helen's eye.' 'Beauty vanishes, however rare, rare it be.' 'Dear dead women, with such hair too.' Trite, I thought, and hackneyed, and I shook them away.

'I must explain about Agnes,' I said swiftly, and plunged into the story, ending with, 'so I can't offer you breakfast in bed. You'd better get up, and you'd better do it now.' They flung back the clothes, obedient as children. I carried the tea-tray away.

I kept a sharp look-out for Mrs Pawsey, and when at last she arrived I shut myself in the kitchen with her and warned her to let fall no incautious word that would betray the true cause of Agnes's going. I asked her to carry on as best she could, promised that she shouldn't be single-handed for long, and said that we'd be out for lunch.

We all went in Dahlia's car into the town because mine

would only seat two inside with any comfort. I was rather glad because with Dahlia driving I had more time to stare at the familiar landmarks which Megan insisted upon hailing with cries of recognition.

'That's where you used to meet us in the summer, Polly,' she said as we flashed past the Green. 'Do you remember the time when we tried to bring you home some ice-cream in a basin? By the time you got it it was like warm custard.'

'And now the ice-cream boy is a familiar figure in every lane, and I'm sure there's not a child in England who thinks that ice-cream is tepid custard. I did for quite a long time. Things change, don't they?'

'Progress,' said Megan. 'Oh, look, Galley Wood, where the oxlips grew. And the gipsy boy's grave. I'd forgotten the gipsy boy's grave. Were there any flowers on it? Did any of you see? We went past so quickly.'

'Some asters,' said Pen in a tight voice.

'Fancy you noticing,' Megan said. And I remembered that Pen had always passed the little mound with averted head. What a number of things I had forgotten until now. Megan's memory was far better than mine; but of course she had lived longer here.

'What is the gipsy boy's grave?' That velvety voice was Dahlia's, of course; and of course Dahlia didn't share our memories; she was in danger of feeling left out.

'It's a story – almost a legend,' I said, 'but you can't just dismiss it, because the flowers always *are* there in due season.'

Pen interrupted me. 'It's a horrible story. But go on, you might as well tell her. We've stirred up all the feeling of it now.'

There was a little pause, and then, thinking that a great deal was being made out of a small matter – and after all it was the kind of thing to interest a visitor to the neighbourhood – I launched out into the story of how, more than a hundred years ago, a gipsy boy had been hired by a farmer to keep some sheep; and how some of the sheep were missing, and the boy, terrified of being accused of sheep-stealing, a hanging offence in those days, had hanged himself rather than report the loss; and how the sheep were found later, wandering in Galley Wood; and how from that day to this somebody, nobody knows who, but it is said to be other gipsies, puts flowers on the suicide's cross-road grave in season, even holly at Christmas-time. 'We lived here for years,' I finished, 'and we, that is, Meg and I, were frightfully interested in it and used to watch. But we never saw anybody putting flowers on it, and nor did any one that I've ever heard of, but they're always there.'

'Yes,' said Dahlia, 'that is an interesting story – and it is horrible too.'

'Lots of horrible things happened in those old days,' said Megan easily. 'Did you ever read that story of the valiant little tailor?'

'Almighty God,' said Pen, addressing the air, 'what have I done?'

'Somebody has taken the Hall for a boarding school, I hear,' I said swiftly as the grey stone gateway fled behind us.

'The Harrisons have gone?'

'Years ago.'

'Do you remember that boy with the black hair who used to stay there? You know, the one who rode so well. We used to go to the Point-to-Point and yearn over him.'

'I didn't,' said Pen.

'Oh, you did. You were worse than I was.'

'Well, anyway, not after you ruined the glamour by calling him Pete, out of some awful book you were gorging at the time.'

'But he was,' said Megan; 'he was just like Pete. And it wasn't an awful book. It thrilled me to the marrow.'

'Then it was a bad book.'

'I don't see why.'

'Well, I wouldn't lay down a hard and fast rule, but I should say that a book ought only to thrill you to the marrow if it reports or describes something that you know, either from the light of personal experience or from the light of knowledge, to be true, so that you can say, "That is just how it happens, or that is just how it did happen." That a book, purporting to be a love-story should thrill the marrow of a girl as ignorant as you were then, as inexperienced, proves, at least to my way of thinking, that it wasn't a good book. It wouldn't thrill you now, would it?'

'No – I suppose not.'

'And why not, do you suppose?'

'Well,' Megan blundered for a bit and then said, 'I suppose you're right. I do know more about men, and women, and so on, now.'

'But that,' I said, irresistibly drawn into their arguments as I had always been, 'isn't the fault of the book, surely. How ought a really good book, say about love, to affect an ignorant young girl, Pen?'

'With a sort of horror, I should say. You see, the girl is all full of dreams and illusions – and people shouldn't write books if they haven't got past the dream and illusionary stage themselves. Therefore what was written out of experience should disgust the inexperienced – as it does. Look at Hemingway and Aldington; people with permanently adolescent minds are disgusted with them still.'

'Your argument would severely restrict the reading that a young girl could do, wouldn't it?'

It was Megan who answered the question, and surprisingly too.

'And rightly,' she said. 'It is that mock stuff that sends you out with all the wrong ideas. You kind of expect a man to be a cross between a cave man and one of Arthur's knights.'

'Pete, in fact?' asked Pen. Meg nodded.

'I wonder where he is now.'

'Who, Pete?'

'No, stupid, the boy with the black hair.'

'Stiffening in the knees and heavy in the saddle wherever

he is,' I said brutally, and then I let my gaze follow Meg's out of the window.

It was a glorious morning, full of mellow sunshine and clear. On many old walls the creepers were blazing, scarlet, amber, and apricot. Here and there a solitary chestnut-tree that had changed colour before the rest – and chestnuts are most individual in their times of budding and changing shade – struck upon the almost incredulous sight in a miracle of yellow that set one thinking of Moses and the burning bush. If one could only arrest the process and preserve it so, with a few leaves scattered on the green grass like trapped sunshine!

The stubble was almost all cleared now, and the ploughs were out, moving slowly with the brown shining furrows turning and lengthening behind them. Even when we reached the outskirts of the town where the raw new houses clustered, the mountain ash-trees drooped their coral berries in redeeming beauty over gates labelled 'Dunromin' and 'Kosy Kot'.

'Twenty minutes,' said Megan, looking at her watch. 'And old Gooch's cart used to take over two hours. We used to get so cold. Do you remember, Pen, when that brat was sick all over your lap and your brand-new handbag and you threw the bag away, contents and all, into a field? I *was* so shocked.'

'Ugh! I remember. There was a half-crown in it too. I wonder if any one found it. I say, Polly, is Cope's bun-shop still in existence?'

'It's still called Cope's, and it looks much the same.'

'We must take home some of those Chelsea buns for tea, mustn't we? I wonder if they're still as sticky.'

'Oh, dear,' Meg sighed. 'I used to eat four straight off. How lovely not to have to consider one's figure. I can hardly imagine what that would feel like.'

'Four would certainly make a bulge on you now,' I said with a glance at the long slim lines of her black coat.

'Still, we'll buy four and eat them solemnly for auld lang syne.'

'We'll buy three for that and one to introduce Dahlia to the joys of gluttony,' I said.

'Where do I park?' asked Dahlia, half turning. I leaned forward to direct her and in a few moments we were tripping over the cobblestones of the ancient Market Place.

'I've got to go to the registry office, and I may be some time,' I said. 'You'd better meet me at the "Castle" at about quarter to one. We'll have our lunch there.'

'Oh, we can occupy ourselves,' said Megan, thrusting one hand into the crook of Pen's arm and drawing Dahlia along with the other. 'I want to walk past the school, and pull a long nose at old Mother Craske's and I'll buy those buns, oh, and heaps of things.'

Her gaiety affected them as it always did people; she'd always been able to make a picnic out of a biscuit and a bottle of ginger-beer, and now, with gloomy Dahlia on one side and sober Pen on the other, she went lightly off down the street and before they turned the corner a shred of laughter blew back at me. For quite the millionth time I caught myself wondering why, in my secret heart, I liked Pen better. And I remembered one of Mother's sayings, one she said at least once a week to Meg, when she was in this kind of mood, 'You'll cry before night.' And often enough it had been true.

At the registry office I had a long session with an optimistic lady who had obviously believed all that the Reckitt's Blue advertisements promise about its white-preserving qualities, and applied what she had read to hair as well as clothes. The only trouble was that she had forgotten, or neglected, to rinse her hair afterwards, and the unreality of her colouring prevented me somehow from taking her very seriously. In that, as it turned out, I was wrong, for she 'fitted me up' – her expression – with a middle-aged woman who filled Agnes's place to a nicety.

On my way to the 'Castle' I left an order with the grocer,

and one with the butcher, and bought a supply of dog food. I then called at the post office to complain mildly that nothing had yet been done about my request for a telephone. By that time it was ten minutes to one and I abandoned the idea I had had of buying stockings, and hurried in an undignified manner to meet my guests. Even then I arrived first, for Meg, who simply could not resist any kind of shop, had been indulging in an orgy, and as the three of them came strolling towards me I could see that they were loaded with small and rather insecurely fastened little packages. Just as they joined me, and Meg was launching out into a description of all they had seen and done, we had to stand aside from the doorway to let out two women, farmers' wives by the look of them, who were coming from the 'Castle' yard. In the old days that had been *the* place to leave your horse and trap, and although the yard and the stables offered awkward and inadequate parking for cars, many people continued to use it from habit in preference to the new car park. These women met Dahlia and the rest of us, and there was that usual over-polite side-stepping and backing that occurs when people meet so. When that was over and our way was clear, one of the women, now behind us, said in a loud country voice to her companion, 'Did you see that, Floss, a nigger!' I had just a hope that Dahlia, almost through the doorway, might not have heard, but her hearing was unusually sharp and a glance at her told me that she had heard all right. Bottomless hell! I thought. I swung on my heel; for a moment a passion of rage almost drove me after the fat red woman in the mangy fur. I could have smashed in her face and torn out her hair with all the pleasure in the world. But what was the use? There was the fact of Dahlia's colour, sticking out, as she herself had said, a mile. Why resent the observation of a fact? But why, oh, why, must it happen today? Just when she was feeling edgy, just when she was in my care.

I stuck my arm through hers, a foolish thing to do, since

it betrayed the fact that I, too, had heard and considered it a matter of sympathy, and said as lightly as I could, 'Well, what do you think of our genuine Tudor inn? Mr Pickwick is supposed to have stayed here.'

Pen lounged over to the framed sketches of Pickwick and Sam Weller, and the rest of them that hung on the wall and said, 'That's an achievement, isn't it? To draw forth that remark from everyone who enters here, and to have them believe it.'

'But it's a fact,' put in Meg. 'He did stay here. They'll show you a bed upstairs that he slept in, and there's a pump in the yard that Sam Weller washed at.'

'Not really,' asked Pen, raising her other eyebrow level with the scarred one.

'Yes, really. You know it's true, Pen. He went to the "Angel" at Bury too, and to the "White Horse" at Ipswich.'

'Who did?'

'Mr Pickwick.'

'There you are, you see. An achievement, as I said.'

Meg stood puzzled for an instant, then she burst out laughing. 'Of course, I see. An achievement indeed.'

We wandered about the room with glasses of rather warm and sticky gin and vermouth in our hands.

'Drinking is frequently sordid now and must have been more so in the past, yet old pubs are romantic, aren't they? I wonder why they should be, more so than houses, I mean?' Pen asked.

'I should think because life passed through them. Houses only shut in the little stories of their occupants. An inn was like the highway,' I proffered.

'Take that, for example.' She pointed to some weapons, rapiers, swords; I didn't know which or whether they actually differed, that hung over the open fireplace. 'They may have killed somebody, ended a life that was full of interest. And curiously enough the very breath I draw to remark upon it may be the one that came out in a gasp as the point went in . . . blown round the world for hundreds of years.'

'Oh, grim,' said Dahlia. 'It might be a very nice breath, if you're going to think that way. The breath that Helen said "Hullo!" with to Leander when he came up all dripping out of Hellespont.'

'Oh, not "Hullo", surely,' said Megan smiling. 'Too dull, she'd have said "*Dar*ling", like that.'

'She more likely said, "Come in and get those wet things off," ' said Pen.

Chatting in this fashion, we went across to the dining-room and dealt, each after her fashion, with the solid good fare provided. I made by far the best meal. Pen never ate much or cared what she ate. Dahlia was still off her food and Megan careful of her figure.

When the coffee came Dahlia looked at her watch, hesitated for a second, and said, 'I think I'll use the telephone, Pour mine, please, white. I shan't be very long.'

She went out with her peculiar lithe walk, and I noticed that the eyes of all the people at the other tables followed her with interest. I realised suddenly that this wasn't the best place in all the world for Dahlia. In a neighbourhood like this, where every one knew every one else even a casual stranger was likely to excite inquisitive interest. Dahlia's difference was bound to be noticed. However, when she returned after an interval of fifteen minutes, during which I had been glad that I hadn't taken her at her word and poured her coffee, she was looking better, relieved almost, as though she had at last made some decision and was glad of it. She drank her almost tepid coffee at a gulp, and then we went to the cinema, there being a matinee as it was market day.

Mrs Pawsey was ready to leave when we arrived. I thanked her for staying and told her that help had been promised for tomorrow. Everything was spick and span; she had even, I saw at a glance, repolished the stove that had suffered at my hands in the morning. The boiler fire was roaring away and I was glad to think that there would be enough hot water for four baths. The meal was ready too; so I took my bath quickly, in order to get out of the way of the others, dressed, put on a thick coat, and set off with the dogs for their evening run in the fields. The peculiarly wide, red, autumn moon, either the Fishers' or the Hunters', I never knew which, was rising over the farthermost hedgerow. The dogs ran scuffling and snorting to and fro, three miles to my one. I walked for quite a long time, thinking about Dahlia and what I was intending to say to her about Roger Hayward. At least I thought about that to begin with. I was calm, resigned, immune, and I was framing sentences that would convince Dahlia that she was fretting over the passing of a shadow ... and I ended in a state of mind where I wanted to fling myself on the bare damp soil and tear up handfuls of it in a rage of frustration and desire and self-hatred. I suppose it was like a fever that comes suddenly to a crisis after the blood has tried in vain to neutralise or annihilate a chance germ. Roger Hayward. R. F. M. Hayward, Esq. I'd written that on about half a dozen envelopes and watched it transform the lifeless paper into something significant and precious. Roger Hayward, whose interests covered a dozen different worlds, and who had invaded mine becase he was a friend of old Worboise, who was making *Island Magic* that we were doing the songs for. Roger had once, years before, lived for about five years in the South Seas and old Worboise, with his incomparable skill in getting something for nothing, was busily picking his brains for information. I will say for old Worboise that he is a devil for information, his is all accurate and firsthand and almost all unpaid for. I paid, I suppose, for the bits he was scavenging that day.

Blast Roger Hayward! I know he's good to look at; but one day, quite soon, he'll be fat, and then his likeness to one of the more decadent Roman Emperors won't be attractive any more. I know he moves with a kind of restrained energy, especially on stairs, that I found wellnigh irresistible; but age and increasing weight will deal with that. I know that he's so utterly natural and frank, so openly selfish, so unashamedly self-centred, that even the people whom he hurts most can never complain that they have been deceived by him. I know that he has a gaiety and a confidence, a breezy lack of conscience that are like a warm fire on a cold night, but what is all that to me?

Those old fellows who wrote the Bible were wise in their generation when they talked about the lust of the eye and the lust of the ear. Dahlia and I were both prey to those lusts, and to a third, the lust of the flesh. For neither of us – and surely not one of Roger's many women – can possibly have been in love with him. No one could love so fundamentally unlovable a person. 'Oh, son of man, according as thou art lovable those thou livest with will love thee.' Who wrote that? With the exception perhaps of his honesty and his gaiety, which both arise, I suspect, from his lack of consideration for other people, he hasn't a single lovable quality. Lust of the eye. And yet he is the last person on earth to be called handsome. His nose is like Punch's, and his mouth is a firm, hard slit. There's too much muscle on his jaw, too; and when he looks at you and desire takes him, you can see the movement of it, as though he were biting on something. God, I didn't know I was so observant!

'There's something about that look,' said Dahlia.

Yes, and it had knocked me endways when I met it first across the table in old Worboise's overheated office. Calculating, flattering, critical, ready to be amused. 'Play with me?' Bluish-grey eyes under thick brows a good deal lighter than his hair. If I could only see them looking at me like that again; if I could only be at the beginning, the delirious, heady beginning once more, I'd see if I couldn't handle it better. No, I wouldn't. I'd flee from that look as I would from an infection. 'If thine eye offend thee, pluck it out.' I wouldn't listen to a word of that talk about palms and moonlight, about lagoons and beachcombers and the music of guitars, with those eyes watching me and weighing me up all the time. I'd go straight out of that office, and I wouldn't wait to be caught up and swept off to lunch with some one I'd never seen till that morning. And I wouldn't listen to a word of that talk that was his special line.

'... the most impossibly flattering things – things you might read or imagine, but never expect to hear spoken,' said Dahlia. Things so blatant that you'd never think any one *would* say them, my mind cried fiercely, but that was only to drown, or try to drown the memory of the things that lazy voice had said.

'Will you take your hat off?'

'Why?'

'Never mind. Take it off. Ah, that's better: exactly like the photograph.'

'What photograph?'

'I don't know. I saw one in a paper. It had under it, "Miss Phyllis Field, Polly to her friends, who is half the Phyllida combine whose songs in *Up and Doing* are taking London by storm." Will you be Polly to me?'

Oh, I oughtn't to have worked! I wasn't virgin. I wasn't even young; and I'm not a romantic or susceptible person. I'd have called myself hard-boiled. And perhaps that held the secret. He was too. There was a directness, a clarity, a ruthlessness about him that appealed to what there was of those qualities in me. And the same things made us laugh. Dozens of times since I saw him last I've been in situations where I could just imagine our eyes meeting for a second before we collapsed into helpless laughter. At those times my nostalgia for him reached its heights.

I stumbled along on the narrow paths between the ploughland and the ditches, raking over the ashes of that affair; my mind occupied all the time by the slightly caricatured figures that memory throws up, caricatured because they are remembered by one or two individual and overemphasised features: Dahlia, Roger, and a blurry figure, Phyllis Field, myself. Myself, a scrap of life housed for a little time in a structure of blood and bones, flesh and glands that appeared to be identity's servant, and was in reality its relentless master. For, just because some of my bones and organs were arranged in a pattern called female, I, the indweller, had developed a passion akin to the hunger for food, for another structure and *its* indweller. Here, personality, is your Waterloo, and here, freewill, your Actium. For clear-sighted and unbeguiled, without tenderness and without a thought beyond the plane of the physical, I yet fell victim to the fevers, the disruptions, the desires that people lump together under the misleading name of love. I never called it so. There may be people who love unselfishly, who do not seek in that name either the flattering of vanity or the assuagement of lust, and only they should use the word. I eschew it. As we did. I don't believe the word was ever mentioned between us. Interest was there, and a certain similarity of mind, the same things amused or disgusted us. But actually the only bond between us was the desire of the flesh. I realised that with a complete insight that startled even me on the very first time I stayed with him – and that was the second time we met. He was still asleep in the morning when I came back from my bath and began quietly to put on the clothes that I had thrown off in a frenzy of impatience a few hours before. I found myself looking at him as at a stranger, impersonally, undesirous. I decided that it must have been curiosity that had brought me there. That was satisfied now, and the spell, I told myself, was broken.

He woke up just as I put on my coat, raised himself on his elbow, and shook back his hair. 'What on earth are you doing?' he asked me.

'I'm going out,' I said foolishly.

'But you must have some breakfast. Why this hurry?'

'I just want to go, that's all.'

'Is anything the matter? You haven't got a conscience?'

That made me laugh. He reached out a hand and said, 'Come here.' I went over and put a hand on his. Now, I thought, angrily, I shall begin to answer again. Bottomless hell, why didn't I go through the door? But I might have been touching wood.

'When'll I see you again?'

'I don't know. I'll ring you,' I said. Then Roger laughed, throwing himself back on the pillow.

'You are the *most* peculiar person. All right, but make it soon.'

I walked along to the garage where I had left my car, and while they were filling her up I went into a place to drink some coffee. And there, quite suddenly, it burst upon me that the measure of this satiety was the measure of my satisfaction. I remembered, most unwillingly, two earlier affairs. For Clifford I had had an enormous deep feeling – or so I thought at the time, and Alec I had admired so much that with him I was always uncertain and diffident. But association with them had never been so complete, there had been gaps that we had tried to fill with talk, with the making of promises and the giving of presents. I realised the utter, rather cynical truth of old Raleigh's words, 'The shallow murmur, but the deep are dumb.' Something, either our maturity, or the affinity of our blood, something purely chemical, no doubt, had driven Roger and me into a unity that needed no words, no promises, no tendernesses, nothing but its own consummation. And from that moment I desired him again.

I knew all the time that from the romantic, the sentimental, the idealistic point of view it was a sorry affair enough. But I didn't mind. I saw it – until I went mad – clearly. I knew that I would never have laid down my life, my identity, or even my comfort on Roger Hayward's behalf; and, without wronging him at all I could make the same denial in his name. Heaps of people, I know, feeeling not much differently would apply the word love to their emotions, blaspheming thereby a word that has led others to the stake, the gallows, and the Cross. But we weren't like that. Our bodies found one another pleasant to look at and listen to and touch; they enjoyed the frenzy of feeling that they were capable of arousing in one another. We knew what we wanted, were able to take it, and lucky enough to enjoy it. And that was all.

Why, then, was I walking now in these dim fields, raging and impotent, prey to a gnawing hunger that I had no means of appeasing? And the answer to that was prompt and simple. Because I was a fool, a natural, congenital, dyed-in-the-wool fool. As long as I knew desire for a beast that must be mastered as well as fed, all was well. And then – ancient damnation – it was as if a lion-tamer had begun treating his charges like domestic pussy cats.

The season was against me too.

That year I was living in a funny poky little cottage that belonged to Maisie. She lent it to people when she didn't want it, and she'd lent it to me for the summer. I hadn't lived in the country since I had left Pedlar's Green, and the magic of it stole away my reason and laid my defences flat as the earth from which the bluebells and the cowslips sprang. It was that perilous season when the beech-trees followed the hawthorn's green and the blossom-time came hard after. I made my brief and only excursion into the cloud-cuckoo-land of the imagination, and I found Roger's name on all the banners that the spring had hung about it.

I fought. I reminded myself that this was the mating season, that something deeper than one's intelligence, and older than the human race was at work within fur and feather and petal in order that next year's sun might shine upon the new life that this season's disturbance would germinate and launch. I knew all that. And I might just as well have read a book of poetry, 'hunting the amorous line, skimming the rest.' Just as well.

On two lilac-tipsy evenings a part of me that was a stranger composed and wrote and posted indiscreet, traitorous screeds. Oh, Cranmer, that right hand of yours, paying in flame for its penmanship, how symbolic it was!

Once, waking in a dawn clamorous with birdsong and

full of rosy cloud, I found myself rebelling against the material aspect of our association – the very thing that had made it rare and tolerable. My imagination, raw and untrained, set to work upon Roger's image, and when it had finished he was no more the philanderer with whom I had chosen lightly to philander for a little while – he was a lonely soul, seeking in many women, and never finding, the satisfaction of his discontent.

God, I can hardly believe it even now. I got to a state where I felt that he had come to me seeking bread and I had given him a stone. And then, instead of letting the dangerous moment pass, I, being a fool, telephoned to the Roger of my imagining, instead of the Roger of actuality who wouldn't have known the bread of the spirit had it been thrust beneath his arrogant nose.

An ill-timed request for a meeting; two letters that should have been destroyed immediately they were written; a stupid telephone conversation – more than enough to evoke that inevitable male reaction. 'Here is another clinging woman who will be a nuisance.' The frail, brittle bark of our mutual self-interest could not cope with the weight of the crumb of sentiment that I brought aboard it, in the time of the cuckoo calling, in the time of the hawthorn blooming, in the time of my folly.

One broken appointment – profusely apologised for – was sufficient to open my eyes.

All hell, I thought. Trying to make a questing soul, a searching pilgrim, out of Roger Hayward. You deserve to be pilloried where every woman you've ever laughed at or pitied could spit at you. I imagined him with one of his other women, immune from me, lapped away in a trance of new desire. Imagine, I said to myself, trying to run a hard head and a soft heart side by side. Poor bloody fool! Ophelia with your head full of lilac and birdsong and night running gently in over the fields of evening all on his account. How could you be so crass, so hackneyed, so jejune?

In a way mine was the victory too. For the perversity, that, incidentally must be hell for people like Roger, who shrink from what is offered and run hot-foot after what is withheld, this perversity swung him me-ward again as soon as I regained my sanity.

There were days of silence between us and then his voice came, in the evening, drawling and caressing over my telephone.

'Darling, I couldn't think what had happened. Why this silence?'

'I've been very busy.'

'Busy as all that? Not a word or a line for days.'

'I haven't noticed a lot from you either.' Foolish, traitorous remark that would yet be spoken.

'You sound rather cross, darling. Are you cross with me?'

'Of course not. Why should I be? I'm just most awfully busy.'

Something I didn't quite catch, it wasn't a very good connection.

'... come up on Thursday, can you?'

'Sorry, but I shan't have a moment this week. I'm going to America on Monday.'

'Where?' And the voice had changed too.

'America, Hollywood.'

'What on earth for?'

'Fun. As a matter of fact I've got a job there.'

'Isn't this all very sudden?' Neglected maiden seeking anodyne to sorrow?

'Not very. I've been angling for it for ages.'

'But why?'

'Wanderlust. Fresh worlds to conquer me and so on.'

'But Polly, I simply must see you before you go. If you are going. I think I could dissuade you.'

'I'd hate to see you try. And I honestly haven't a minute.'

'I'll run down.' Gosh! How he'd grumbled on the two occasions when he had made that journey.

'But I'm leaving here tonight.'

'Then you're coming to London?'

'No. I'm going to my sister.' A lie, but why despise so useful an ally?

'You are the cussedest person! How long shall you be there?'

'God knows. I say, I can hear my kettle boiling over on to the floor. Good-bye, Roger.'

'Damn the kettle, I say, Polly, what about . . .'

I replaced the receiver. The kettle was not boiling. I had not got a job in America . . . but I had proved that I wasn't going to be a bore to Mr Hayward. And later on I did get a job. I turned at the end of the next field and shouted to the dogs who came up breathless out of the darkness and were now content to follow me back to the house.

All that was more than two years ago, and except for one letter, forwarded to me, a few casual references from various people who knew us both, and, last night, Dahlia's admissions, I had heard nothing of Roger Hayward since. I'd been busy, and lucky, I'd met a lot of people and made some money. I hadn't missed a meal or a night's sleep to my knowledge because of him. And here I was smitten again with the fever I imagined cured. I gripped my hands and gritted my teeth. I've got rid of this obsession once and I will again. Before I go back into the house, my peaceful, happy house, I will be calm and whole again. Roger Hayward liked me to laugh with and to sleep with occasionally. I liked him for the same reasons. I became 'intense', he was bored, I saw my error and we parted. Has he ever moped about in a moonlight field feeling as though vultures were tearing at his vitals? No. Then why should I? Suppose I'd never met him, should I have been conscious of something lacking in my life? Of course not. Why don't I now remember Clifford who had so much more of my life and was so much better a person? Or Alec? Or . . . or . . . any of them? Why can I remember the very way he walks, with a kind of chained vigour, especially when he goes up and down stairs? Simply because he happens to be the most vigorous and perhaps the most physically healthy person that I have known . . . and for that reason my body, blindly, biologically wise, craves for his. I'm like a cow. And Dahlia is like a cow. We're all cows. So here I am, with a whole, sound, independent body and an unsentimental mind. I should like to go to bed again with Roger. I should like a million dollars. Why should the failure to get one thing send me ripstitching about the countryside and the other not cost me a sigh? Why? Because failure in the emotional field is a thing that people sentimentalise over from habit; half our songs and books prove that. I will not be a partner to it. I will not be a cow.

V

WE struck the lane again about a couple of hundred yards above the gate: and immediately I was thrown into something like panic by the sight of a car's lights approaching. None of the dogs was on a lead and the puppies were not yet completely obedient. There was no house but my own in the lane, and we had never met traffic there before. I called the dogs, and slipped my hand through two or three collars, and stood back on the rough grass by the side of the lane, waiting for the thing, whatever it was, to pass. It came very slowly, and then stopped. It occurred to me that it was some one who had missed the way, and as I walked forward, rounding the vehicle, and stooped over the dogs, I saw by the light of the taillamp a London taxi identification plate, which confirmed my belief. I reached the entrance to my drive just as a tall, massive figure in a pale overcoat turned, with a hand on the gate, and said, in a deep, musical voice,

'Wait here. I'll see if this is the place.'

Block began to bark and in a moment everything was pandemonium, through which I bellowed, 'It's all right, they won't hurt you. What place are you looking for?'

'Pedlar's Green,' said the musical voice.

'Oh,' I said, 'whom do you want?'

'Miss Dahlia Whitman.' There was something vaguely familiar to me in that velvety, trombone-like voice, but for the life of me I couldn't place it. 'She is staying with Miss Field.'

'Yes,' I said. 'Well, this is Pedlar's Green, and I'm Miss Field. Dahlia is here. Come in.'

We had reached the door and I threw it open quickly. The man passed me, I pushed back the dogs, shut the door and straightening myself, looked into the face, the broad, black face of Chester Reed, the negro pianist.

For a moment I was staggered. I must still have been dazed by my thoughts or I should have recognised that voice, noticed, even under the shadow of the trees the lack of light about the face. Then I could have pretended that I was the maid so that I could have spoken to Dahlia before I admitted that she was here. Fool that I was.

I suspected that Dahlia would be furious. Chester Reed had been rather a bother to her in the past, hanging around, asking her out, sending her flowers. She always protested that she couldn't bear the sight of him, and I could understand that. 'The rock whence ye are hewn,' I used to think. I looked at him rather curiously as he stood in my hall. His close-cropped kinky hair shone under the gentle light of the shaded bulb. There was dignity in his face, and kindliness, and he looked superbly happy. He was a fine man, too, as big as Roger, that was my involuntary thought. One part of my mind thought all these things while the rest registered surprise. I must behave as though he were just one of the people we knew, come to see Dahlia. I held out my hand. 'I'm so sorry I didn't recognise you before,' I said, with truth. 'If you'll wait in here for a moment I'll fetch Dahlia.

Have you come from London? What a journey. Will you have a drink?' He shook his head and smiled. Happy, easy, a superbly healthy animal I thought, noting the firmness of his flesh, the brightness of eye, the magnificent teeth. I closed the door and went across to the lounge where only Penelope was reading by the fire. 'I suppose Dahlia is upstairs,' I said.

'Changing her frock, I think,' said Pen. 'She's beautiful, isn't she?'

'I think so,' I said rather absently. 'Some one's come to see her, and I don't think she'll be very pleased.'

But Dahlia, when I told her, seemed neither displeased nor very surprised.

'He's a quick worker,' she said, twiddling the little C-shaped curls into place over her brow.

'I can't think how he found out where you were. But you needn't see him if you don't want to. I can get rid of him for you.' I was quite ready to remedy my mistake in letting him in.

'I'll see him,' said Dahlia. 'What frock shall I wear?'

'Depends what impression you want to make.'

'Oh, a good one.' I opened the wardrobe and ran my hand over the dresses, multicoloured, that hung there. I had my hand on a cyclamen-coloured affair with long filmy sleeves when Dahlia reached over my shoulder and snatched the dress that she had worn the evening before. Pulling it over her head and patting its folds she said, 'This makes me look as black as your boot. Don't stare. I knew it. There! Now where have you put him?'

'Dining-room.'

'How'd he get here? He had his licence suspended last week, and trains make him sick.'

'There's a taxi outside, ticking up a nice little bill.'

'Then it'll be a short session,' said Dahlia, and glided away downstairs.'

But it wasn't. I hung about the kitchen for a long time, playing put-and-take with the items of the meal, trying to keep everything hot without spoiling any of it. The soup thickened, and I thinned it down with milk as long as it lasted, then I used water, finally I considered that it would be uneatable anyway and pulled it off the stove. But it still smelt like tomato soup I noticed, and my mind drew, without arresting my whole attention, a likeness between my watered soup and Dahlia's coloured blood. I sauntered into the lounge where Megan and Penelope were talking with grave faces about some matter that they dropped as soon as I entered. We drank sherry, and I explained all about Dahlia and Chester Reed, as far as I knew. Pen said, 'I should think she phoned him this morning. She came back looking like somebody who had taken a fence and was glad about it.'

'Of course,' I said, 'I hadn't thought of that.'

Presently a thought struck me. Ought I to offer him some food? I looked at Megan. She'd lived in Africa and people like that often had awfully strong feelings about colour. I remembered a scene at a tennis club to which my aunt had belonged. A visiting team of eight had two Indians in it. The ladies of the club had prepared tea and were about to serve it. One of them, the wife of a retired Indian civil servant, picked up a plate of sandwiches and was approaching the guests when her husband struck it out of her hand, and said, 'You shall not wait on them!' I was only a child at the time but the scene, and the general pretence that the plate had fallen by accident, and that the words had not been spoken, had stuck in my mind. I had been so surprised too, for the man was usually so meek and inoffensive and subservient to his wife. He must, I now reflected, have felt very strongly upon the matter. Could I ask Megan to sit down to dinner with Chester Reed? Yet there was Paul Robeson to consider, and the Aga Khan . . . surely no one would ban them from their table. Oh, dear. I said in a voice made small by my ignorance and embarrassment, 'Do you think I ought to offer him some grub. . . . I mean, would you mind?'

Megan came back from some far-off place to which she had gone when the conversation with Pen was broken, and said vaguely, 'Oh, I don't mind a bit. I'm not like that.' It was Pen who said, 'Oh, must you? I hate negroes, not for themselves, but they give me such awful thoughts, all about slaves, and *Uncle Tom's Cabin*, and lynchings in the Southern States. Their very faces have the melancholy of the wronged.'

'Why wrong this one still further?' Meg asked.

Pen laughed. 'I know,' she said, 'it's nonsense. Part of my mania, like the gipsy's grave. Ask him by all means.'

As she spoke the door opened and Dahlia came in.

'I'm awfully sorry, Polly, to have been so long.'

'That's all right. Where's Mr Reed?' I said.

'He's gone.'

'Oh. I was just going to ask him to stay for dinner.'

'Were you really? How nice of you. Anyway, he has to play somewhere at half-past ten. He'll have a rush as it is. We've just got engaged.' She tacked on the last sentence hurriedly, and thrust her left hand towards me, exposing the ring with a diamond about the size of a threepenny bit that blazed there. 'I didn't really want this,' she gabbled on. 'We're going to be married as soon as possible; but he'd bought it this afternoon. I couldn't not have it, could I?'

'It's beautiful,' said Megan. 'Why didn't you want it?'

Dahlia raised one shoulder. 'Oh, I dunno. It seems such an English thing to do somehow.' And for the first time she looked me full in the face. Something – was it Dahlia's self, or the three-quarters white in her, or merely something I imagined? – looked out at me and cried 'Betrayed'.

I thought, she rang him up this morning, just after that woman had dropped the careless 'nigger' in her hearing. It was the merest impulse; but Chester Reed went out at once and bought this 'English' symbol which translated the impulse into accomplished fact. And that is the end of Dahlia.

'Congratulations,' I said in a voice that I vainly tried to infuse with warmth. 'Come on, we'll drink to you quickly and then we'll have this belated grub.'

VI

I CLOSED my bedroom door, settled Block and Velvet with a final pat, and dropped down on my bed. It had been, I thought, the longest day I remembered. Just to think back to the time when the sun broke into the kitchen was like remembering something ten years ago. I felt tired and hollow and troubled. And I had too, a most unreasonable feeling that I mustn't be tired, or hollow or troubled. I felt like some one who has been left in charge of three invalids. Only, there are things to do for invalids, useful, helpful things.

I undressed slowly, washed myself, gave my hair its regulation twenty strokes with a stiff brush, put on my pyjamas. And all the time I kept thinking about Dahlia. It seemed that every time I thought of her I could see a shadow behind her, soft and insinuating, waiting, ready to engulf her, the huge black shadow of Chester Reed.

It's nothing to make a tragedy of, I told myself firmly. Possibly he appeals to some atavistic streak in her. Anyway, plenty of perfectly white women marry negroes. I must not think about this in the traditional, prejudiced manner. But I'm not. Whoever she had got engaged to today I should want to register some protest, because I should know that she wasn't in love with him. People shouldn't make loveless marriages . . . at least a few hard-bitten mercenary people can, and make success of it, but not people like Dahlia.

I looked at my bed, thought backwards to six o'clock that

morning, and forward to six o'clock the next. . . . But I resisted the bed's invitation. I gave myself a shake, pulled on my dressing-gown, and went along to Dahlia's room. She hadn't started to undress. The curtains were pulled back from the window and shuddered in the strong current of cool air that came through the open casement. Between them Dahlia was kneeling on the window seat, staring out of the window. She turned her head as I entered and the whole of beauty was held for a moment in that slight movement, the lift and turn of the head, the flexing of the muscles in the slender back. She turned back to the window as she said, 'Hullo, I was expecting you.'

'Oh? Well, I damn nearly didn't come.'

'Oh, Polly,' her voice was teasing, 'you couldn't resist an opportunity of wrestling with me for my own good. Could you?'

'I both could and can,' I said rather sharply. 'I don't want to wrestle with you, and I do want to go to sleep. So good night.'

'Oh, Polly, please. I didn't mean it. Come here and look at the moon for a minute.'

'Looking at the moon makes people mad,' I said, but I went and knelt beside her on the window seat. The moon that had risen so wide and red – how long ago? – was small now and high, a silver shield held aloft over the dark fields of cloud.

'Do you believe it, that it's just a dead world, reflecting the light of the sun?'

'I've no reason to think otherwise.'

'Then it's the female isn't it? I never realised before how right it is to call the moon "she" and the sun "he". Awfully right.'

That called for no answer and I made none.

'You're right about the madness, Polly. You can stare and stare until what you are and what you do, what you think and feel are of no importance at all. Can't you?'

'No,' I said truthfully; 'it's only the moon, after all. What is important to me is important to me, and would be if there were suddenly six moons in the sky.'

Twisting her head slightly, she looked at me thoughtfully.

'You're a lucky devil, Polly, you know. You've got a lot of sense, just sound sense. Have you ever fallen badly for anybody?'

'Dozens of times.'

'Incredible. Has it ever made you do anything utterly foolish?'

'Amongst other things it sent me to America.'

'Father in Heaven! I never guessed that that was why. Still, that was a good move, really, wasn't it? Not to be compared with what I've done today.'

'That's what I came here to talk about, fool,' I said. 'But I can't talk with this wind blowing or with you staring out of the window.' I swung the open casement to with a crash and tugged the curtains across. Then I said bluntly, 'Look here, Dahlia, if you saw a hat you wanted and couldn't have it for some reason, that wouldn't embitter the rest of your life.'

'I'm no good at parables,' Dahlia said stiffly.

'Well, that's what you're doing. Just because you can't have Roger Hayward you've picked on the most unsuitable person in the world for you.'

'You can't compare picking a husband with choosing a hat.'

'Why the hell not? It's exactly the same. You pick something that takes your eye, suits you, and looks as if it'll please you. And being disappointed over a man is no more than being disappointed over a hat.'

'What rubbish!' said Dahlia. 'There's your heart to consider – and your soul.'

'Oh, spare me,' I said. 'And, anyway, if your heart and soul drive you to marry a man you do not love you'd do better not to consider them.'

'But that isn't the only why.'

'What do you mean?'

'I mean that isn't the only reason – Roger isn't – or even the chief one. You heard this morning, didn't you?'

'Heard what?'

'What that woman said.'

'Oh, what of that? They're all ignorant clods round here.'

'Maybe. But an ignorant clod often says what other people only think. You needn't pity me, Polly. There's quite a lot of vanity in it. I thought, "Well, there's one person on this earth to whom I'm white." So I went and rang him and asked if his offer was still open and it was. So there you are. He makes lots of money, and he's generous, good-natured, and crazy about me.'

'Poor deluded devil!'

'Why?'

'So nice for him, isn't it, to be married like that, by a person who, a fortnight ago, found him about as useful as a sick headache. You aren't in love with him, that's why, noodle.'

'That's not his fault, is it? It's my fault. If Chester were white would you be so concerned?'

'Oh,' I said wearily, 'we're not getting anywhere. Dahlia, I don't want you to marry Chester Reed. I'm specially concerned now because you took that silly ignorant word to heart. Don't you see that if you do this you'll have given that woman power over you, let her influence your life? Whereas if you ignore it, it might never have been spoken. After all, it can't be the first time, things being as they are, that you've had to face something of the kind. Why mind this time?'

'Oh, because of Roger, I suppose. I'm really all on edge. I just want to tear my hair and scream.'

'Well do. Nobody'd mind. You might feel a lot better.'

For some reason that I could not myself exactly understand, I had spoken all this time harshly, with a minimum of sympathy. But now, looking at her suddenly and seeing the strain and misery on her face and the littleness of her, I was smitten to the heart. I took both her cold little hands in mine. 'Listen to me,' I said. 'You think I'm hard, I know. I've been trying to *sting* you out of this thing. Now I ask you, Dahlia, at least not to do anything in a hurry. Stay here with me for a bit. Then, when the weather gets really bad, we'll go somewhere where there's some sun. And you'll get over Roger Hayward. Believe, I *know*, he's only a passing infection of the blood.'

'Oh,' said Dahlia, as one upon whom a great light breaks, 'so that is how you know. Oh, my God, how richly funny! Oh, yes, do by all means let's stay here together and form a new order, an enclosed order, Little Sisters of Frustration. We could get a copy of that bronze Sheldrake did of him, and set it up on high and cry, "Holy, holy, holy," in the night watches.' She laughed suddenly, a high, staccato peal that caught my breath.

'Hush,' I said. And when she went on laughing I raised my voice and shouted, picking on the one shred of sense in the whole hysterical outburst, 'Then you will stay? I'll get rid of Chester for you.'

She was calm just as suddenly.

'It isn't any use, Polly. I am going to marry Chester. I want to. Despite all you may think and say it's the most sensible thing, really. He wants me, and I don't see why somebody shouldn't get something out of this. And I do like him. We can understand one another. And he's a man. After Roger I want a man, at least, and how many are there? Frankly, I'm as lecherous as a tomcat, you know, and I've got to cater for that somehow. Don't you give it another thought, Polly. I'm not worth it, truly. There's only one thing I want to do now, and that is . . . '. She got up suddenly and went with her strange panther tread to the dressing-chest that stood on the far side of the bed. I watched her. She opened a drawer and took out a photograph, unframed, still in its folder of stiff paper. She dropped the folder on the floor at her feet and fumbled in her manicure case for a pair of pointed scissors.

She was going to cut it to pieces. Without seeing it I knew

that it was a photograph of Roger. Where had she got it? I'd never had one. Something in me wanted to cry out, 'Let me look at it for a second.' With a feeling akin to food hunger I longed for one sight of that hard, unkind face. Had they caught that alert eye, that thin-lipped mouth, ready with sneer or smile, that arrogant nose? I crushed down the request. I would not be like a child, pressing its nose against a pastrycook's window. Dahlia said, in a still, quiet voice, the lowest note on a mellow fiddle, 'How much civilisation has helped barbarians. Once on a time this would have taken ages of work in clay or tallow and hair. And now . . .'.

Was it pure fancy, or did the room darken and draw itself together in sudden premonition of evil? Was it pure fancy or had Dahlia darkened, too? And why did I think of forests and vile things crawling? I said, 'Dahlia, stop it,' but my voice did not reach her. Holding the photograph in one hand and the bright scissors poised in the other, she said clearly:

'Roger Hayward, may you fall into the pit that your own lust has dug. May all that any woman has suffered through you come back a hundredfold.' And she drove the scissors clean through the cardboard.

I said foolishly, 'That's silly. He can't help himself. He only obeys his nature.'

'As I do,' said Dahlia. She twirled the scissors so that the photograph whirled like a paper windmill and then fell to the floor.

'That'll fix him,' she said with horrid certainty.

'You don't seriously believe that that mumbo-jumbo has any power,' I protested.

'Wait and see,' said Dahlia. She came round the foot of the bed. 'I must go tomorrow and see about things and get rid of my flat. It's been lovely of you to have me, Polly, and I'm sorry to be such a bore. Good night.'

She held up her face. But I had seen, as the scissors went home, the gleam of her eyes and the flash of her teeth.

Fiendish. I couldn't kiss her. I ducked my cheek so that it touched the peak of her hair.

I thought of why I had come there; and I shrugged the thought away. After all, Dahlia wasn't the first woman to marry a man she did not love. Sometimes it worked.

'Good night,' I said flatly. And as I looked at her before leaving, something – was it Dahlia's self, or the three-quarters white in her, or something I merely imagined? – looked out at me and cried 'Betrayed'.

PART II
Going

I

WAKING next morning with the sunlight lying across the foot of my bed and spilling pools of light on the floor, I lay for a little while smoothing out my mind, pressing out, as it were, the impression that Dahlia's affairs had made on me. After all, I could do nothing about them now, and to be saddened by them was foolish and futile. She would go to London and she would marry Chester Reed and that was that. What I had to think about was whether she would still work with me. That, I thought, as I kicked back the covers and made a hasty toilet before tackling the early morning tasks, was the real thing, the only thing that really mattered between Dahlia and me. What did fondness matter? Why the very word, in its true sense, meant foolish. And I was too old, too battered by many contacts, to let fondness for a person whom I could not control cast even a momentary shadow over a day when I might live and be happy. It was in that mood that I started the day.

Just before Dahlia left a tall thin woman, dressed in black and carrying a large cardboard suit-case, arrived and announced that she was Miss Finch, and had been sent from the registry office. I took her into the kitchen, introduced her to Mrs Pawsey, and then showed her Agnes's old room. I wondered, as I looked at her gaunt, ramrod-straight body and long flat feet whether Kipling, who so clearly defined the born cook type, would have allowed her to make him a piece of toast, but she settled down to the discussion of the day's food in a capable and fairly amiable manner, and I hoped for the best.

I went round to the barn with Dahlia to get out her car.

She had run it in very awkwardly on the previous evening and muddled the exit so badly that I said, 'Here, let me do it. If you're going to bungle like this all the way your licence will be suspended too.'

'There are days when I can't drive, or do anything at all. This is one of them, but a special Providence watches me on those occasions.'

'You'd better not go,' I said doubtfully. 'Stay just another day. I seem hardly to have seen you, what with the chores and people coming and going. Do stay.'

'I can't, darling. I promised I'd be back today. But I'll see you soon, won't I? There're the rest of *Slave's Saga* and all those songs for *Patchwork Paradise*, you know. All this,' she dismissed the situation with a wave of her hand, 'won't make any difference to our working together, will it?'

'Well, thank God for that. I was wondering.'

'Oh, but you needn't, Polly. You know – don't you – that nothing, nothing would ever make any difference to that. I'm yours. In fact, apart from gratitude, I think you're the only person that I've any real affection for. If I weren't such a worthless character I'd be willing to spend the rest of my life with you.'

She looked at me with such sincerity in her eyes that I was uncomfortable, thinking as I did of my own thoughts about her that morning.

'Here, drive your own car,' I said.

She shuffled along into the driver's seat and settled the skirt of her coat over her knees.

'I've left something on your bed,' she said with a peculiar little smile.

'Thank you,' I said.

'Wait till you've seen it.'

The girls had come down to the front gate to see her off. I joined them and we stood there waving and calling out farewells, to which I added, 'Be careful.'

'I will. Good-bye. I have enjoyed myself. I'll write....'

She put in her gear with a noise like tearing calico and shot off down the lane.

'Well,' I said, 'I hope her Providence is on the job today, she'll need it.'

Megan closed the gate.

'Remember how Mother used to hate us to swing on this gate?'

'And now it's Polly's and you could swing on it as much as you like, you don't want to. Life is like that,' said Pen.

'Just for that I'm going to have one,' said Megan. She opened it wide, perched on the lowest bar, and with a loud cry thrust off. The gate crashed to and she jumped down, brushing her hands.

'Well, I wonder what possible pleasure we got out of that. I suppose all kids are crazy.'

We dawdled back to the house. I had a feeling that with Dahlia's going something had closed in on the three of us. What it was I had no idea, and as I hate feelings that I can't explain I thrust it away.

About ten minutes later I went upstairs to lay out sheets for Miss Finch's bed, and going past my own door remembered Dahlia's words. In the middle of my eiderdown lay the photograph of Roger with the gaping hole in the jacket about where the heart would be. There was a piece of the cover with it, and scrawled on it in thick pencil were the words, 'May you be the woman.'

'Damn and blast!' I said aloud, and turning the thing plain side uppermost, I tore it into shreds. I went down the back stairs and dropped the pieces into the kitchen stove. I should have slapped Dahlia hard if she'd been anywhere near. Then I thought that I was taking the whole thing far too seriously. It was funny, really, all this cursing and wishing and not daring to look at a pictured face. I shuffled that off too, and smiled as I went through and asked Pen and Meg, 'Now, is there anything you'd like to do?'

Megan, with her unfailing flair for doing the 'right' thing, answered my question with another asked in a quiet voice. 'Have you put any flowers on the grave?'

Slightly startled, I said, 'No, of course not. Ought I to have done?'

'Oh, I do think so. Of course I know it's kept trimmed and so on, but now that you're living here there ought to be flowers on it. Whatever will people think?'

'I'm afraid that pretty little problem never even occurred to me. After all, there haven't been any flowers there for eighteen years.'

'I don't believe you've even been near the churchyard at all.'

'Perfectly right. I haven't.'

'You really are the most amazing creature.'

'But why? Simply because I don't do something that would be certain to either bore me or depress me, although actually I never even thought about it. We'll go now if you like.'

'I think we'd better. Can we take some flowers from the garden? And we shall need a bowl of some sort; something heavy enough to withstand the wind and deep enough to hold a good lot of water.'

'I think you are the amazing creature,' I said, preparing to go in search of the well-defined receptacle. 'What do you say, Pen?'

'I'll come with you,' said Penelope, evading the question.

By the time we had reached the churchyard my old dissatisfaction with myself had convinced me that it was indeed most unnatural of me not to have come here before. I filled the bowl I had chosen at the pump in the wall and then stood back, while Megan, on her knees, most correct in demeanour, arranged the sprays of Michaelmas daisies and the rather scraggy chrysanthemums and asters, which were all that the garden afforded. I looked at the names on the headstone: Arthur William Field, who had been dead for eighteen years and had been sixty when he died; Catherine Mary Field, who had predeceased her husband by two years and had been fifty years of age. Father, whom we had liked very well and laughed at for his unpunctuality and absent-mindedness; Mother, whom we had respected and feared a little because of her sharp tongue. A man and a woman, who, out of their loving, one supposed, though the thought was strange, had created the three people who stood here now in the sun of an October morning. Bones now, and names on a headstone and the faintest of memories in the three minds of their children. I at any rate had never understood either of them.

I knew that Father had once been well-to-do, and had idled away his days reading and collecting books, visiting strange places, and writing verses more remarkable for scholarship than beauty. Faced with penury through some mismanagement of money that even he never thoroughly understood, he had taken to farming in the middle years of his life, not because he knew anything about it, but because he liked living in the country and could not bear organisation of any kind. That was how it was that we had come to live at Pedlar's Green when I was a child of about two. Mother had far more iron in her. Bred in idleness and comfort, she had never flinched in the face of changed circumstances, and my only memory of her is that of a busy bustling woman who knew the prices of eggs and chickens, the value of the calves, and exactly what Father ought to get for the pigs. Had she despised him? Did his inefficiency, his unpunctuality, his serene imperturbability exasperate? There was never a sign of it in her behaviour. Perhaps his academic mind exacted from her practical one the tribute of respect and admiration that practical people pay, all the world over, to something that is just beyond their strong but limited grasp. Or it may have been the other way round. Perhaps they were a perfect pair. Perhaps they were very happy. And their happiness, or their differences, their secret hopes and fears, their egoism, their very identities had ended here, under this curtain of smooth turf and that was all.

I shuffled uncomfortably as Megan, still on her knees,

pulled a spray, settled a flower, snipped off a leaf. It was to avoid thoughts like this that I had ignored the churchyard; the ignoring had been unconscious, certainly, but it had been wise. What was the use of hanging above a tomb? Whom did we serve by remembering? Forget them, forget all the dead who trod the ground and used the moment that we have now inherited. There is food to be bought, and drink to be enjoyed; over in Stoney there are shops where we can buy things. I want to feel the rush of air and the thrill of speed when the needle touches fifty.

I said to Megan, 'Come on. You won't improve on that.'

'Don't grudge a moment,' said Penelope, answering my mood rather than my words; 'they used to sit up o' nights when we were young.'

I set off down the path. The thought wouldn't be borne. And the comparison was faulty. It was not to the living but to the dead that I was grudging. But I didn't trouble to explain.

We dawdled back to the house in silence. I couldn't think of anything to say, Penelope was as quiet as usual, and Megan was muted. There is no other word for it. Her face had a strange, withdrawn look, and I had an uncomfortable feeling that it hadn't been an attitude, after all, that had taken her to the churchyard. Perhaps she did have deep, warm feelings under all her gaiety and poses. And I'd been unsympathetic! I sighed to myself. I'd offered both Dahlia and Megan all that I had yet they seemed all the time to be making dumb demands for something I hadn't got. Yet I knew that if Pen and I had, for some reason, broken down the eighteen-year-old defences and stood there shedding tears over that grave, Megan, after joining us in our weeping, would have been the first to recover, would have offered us words of comfort, her arm, her handkerchief. Then the full circle would have been described, the tribute would have been paid, and Megan would have had a sense of fulfilment. It was all too silly. I broke silence with, 'Shall we go to Stoney now?'

And then Megan put the last elegant touch upon her picture of visiting the past in the correct manner, and said, 'Not this morning. It's so nice. I want to go blackberrying.'

'It's too late in the year,' I said promptly.

'Much too late,' Pen seconded. 'It's after the Equinox when the devil looks over the bushes and blights them all.'

'Never mind. Let's go out on the brakes like we used to. I've thought about doing it every autumn since I did it last.'

'All right,' I said, 'if that's your fancy. Must you have a basket and a crook stick, or will a paper bag do?'

The place that we called 'the brakes' was a piece of waste land, very little good even for grazing. The soil was sandy and there were clumps of wild thyme and outcrops of bracken amongst the grass. It was scattered with blackberry bushes and low scrubby hawthorn-trees, so that it was like a series of grassy passages and little rooms with living walls.

Once upon a time it had been a favourite place for playing in. Penelope and Megan used to take up their abode in two adjoining nooks and pretend that they were neighbours. They had washing days and cooking days and neighbourly quarrels and reunions. There was, however, only one of those domestic completions – children, and that was myself. So one time I was Penelope's child and the next Megan's. A large doll played, so to speak, opposite me. They quarrelled very often about whose turn it was to have me. I always sided with Pen in these arguments. I liked her better, even then. Sometimes our combined evidence resulted in her having me as many as three times running.

Once in the brakes we were sheltered from the wind and conscious of the gentle warmth that was left in the sunshine. It *was* late in the year for blackberrying, the berries fell at a touch, and those we salvaged collapsed into purple mush that stained our fingers and the paper bags. I was rather sorry that in the early days of my living there I had never once thought of this once-so-looked-forward-to pastime. I'd always loved blackberrying-time. There had always been a strange charm about the season, the imminence of change. There was, too, a sense of luckiness about finding a thickly fruited clump, a special warm *black* taste about the berries themselves. It's difficult to explain exactly. Either you enjoy grubbing about for blackberries and nuts and primroses or you don't. But I have heard most surprising people admit a weakness for that kind of thing – women with sophisticated-looking, white hands who can't resist digging up celandines with a nail-file.

I could have blackberried in the brakes by myself quite happily, I'm sure of that. And I could have taken my spoil home and been gluttonous over the pie, the jelly, or the jam, and never given a sorry thought to the fact that we three had had such merry, appetite-raising times there, three lanky children with scratched hands, stained mouths, and plucked holland frocks. But today it seemed for a moment, as I stretched out my hand to the plucking, that they couldn't be gone, those children. They must still be there, gloating over good finds, calling to one another through the gaps in the bushes, yelping to invite sympathy over scratches.

We were lucky, I thought, to have been country bred; to have known the joys of nutting and primrosing in the woods, to have been allowed to try our hands on softened teats at the end of the milking, and to have ridden the cart-horses that had such surprisingly sharp ridgy spines, despite the breadth of their backs. We'd been lucky too, to start off with bodies fortified by fresh air and plenty of milk and eggs and butter. God, I thought, I have a mercenary mind! And just then Megan came round a bush with a most peculiar expression on her face, and said to me, in a voice between tears and laughter, 'Do you remember the wash days? And the day when I took off your liberty bodice to wash with the doll's things, and you got a cold and Mother was so cross . . . '. Her face worked for a moment, and then she dropped the bag she was holding and bowed her face in her hands. Some tears splashed down between her fingers. Bloody hell, I said to myself, that's torn it! But even then I didn't think. . . .

'You were a fool ever to come here,' Pen said harshly.

'It's nothing to cry about, Meg,' I added, calling up my difficult kindness again.

She stood there, bowed over her hands, with the tears running down and her slim shoulders shaking with racking sobs while Pen and I stared at one another in helpless consternation.

At last I went to her and put my arm round her shoulders, bracing her against the impact of her sorrow. She was small, I realised, smaller than Dahlia, to whom I was always so kind. To Megan I was seldom kind; she had evoked admiration, not pity, from me – until now.

'Don't,' I said awkwardly. 'What is it, Meg? Is anything wrong? Tell me, tell us. We'll put it right for you. Darling, don't cry like that, it's so bad for you.'

She drew a deep quivering breath and I felt her body stiffen. Now it was coming. What was it? And would it be anything that we could cope with? Was it a love-affair? Was she in some trouble about Henry?

The breath she had drawn came out in a long miserable sigh, and then she said in a suprisingly calm voice, 'Oh God, I was mad to come here. Mad.'

'But why?' I asked in genuine bewilderment. 'I thought you'd like it. You can go away again, darling, if you don't like it here.' I was remembering how boredom could always drive her butterfly soul to desperation, how sometimes in the middle of something that she had seemed to be liking she would spring up and say, 'Oh, I'm so bored I could die.' I thought, perhaps, the quietude of Pedlar's Green had worked like that already on her. I was not prepared for her to turn and say, 'It isn't that I don't like it. I wanted to come. And really, it doesn't. . . . Oh, it's the years, the time, the knowing that life is over . . . '.

'But Megan – ' A dreadful thought struck me. I remembered that haggard look she had before her face was done up. Perhaps she was ill. Maybe that was why she was so thin. Perhaps she had come over alone and gone to London to consult a doctor, perhaps he had told her something dreadful.

I tightened my arm around her, but she shook herself free and said in that same calm, dead voice, 'Don't mind me. I'm mad. I can't explain it. It just comes over me at times and I just can't bear it. I wish I could die now and not have to face it any more.'

'Face what, Megan? Are you ill?'

'In my mind I am.' She looked at me, haggard and appealing, her eyes smudged with tears and her powder streaky. A silly quotation slipped through my mind, 'Canst thou administer to a mind diseased?' I glanced at Pen, passing on to her the appeal that Meg had made to me. Pen responded.

'Come on,' she said in her dry voice. 'This is a damn silly thing to be doing, haunts of childhood, and all that. Let's get down to the house and Polly will fix you a drink and you can make up your face and you'll feel better.'

'I'll never feel better. I've been making up my face and having drinks for years in order to forget it. It won't be forgotten. Every day is a day lost, and age sets in and the grave is waiting.'

I had never heard anything approaching this from Megan before. I was dumb.

'Well,' said Pen. 'What of it? We all know that, and it's the same for everybody.'

'I know that. What I don't know is how people bear the thought. Think of us. Just yesterday it seems we were running about here with all the future before us, and now here we are, not Polly, perhaps, so much, but you and I, Pen, spent, with no future left. We've used all the life that we're going to have. What we were born and reared for, over, done, finished.'

'You just have to accept that, and not dwell on it. Other people don't.'

'I've never even thought about it,' I put in, foolishly.

Megan turned to me.

'I usen't to. God knows, there never was a less thoughtful or introspective person than I was. And then one day it just happened. At least it was in the night. I woke up and I could hear Henry breathing in the other bed, the way people do when they're asleep. And I realised suddenly that every breath he drew meant one less to draw. I was frightfully keen on Henry then, that was why it hit me so. And then I thought it was the same for me, for everybody. We were all dying slowly. Nothing could stop it, not love, not anything. And the day would come quite soon when love even would be unthinkable between the old bodies we'd have then. And everything I've thought or done since has been coloured by that thought. I tell you I'm mad.'

'Oh, no,' I said. 'I should think it's simply that your nerves are out of order. You ought to see somebody about it.'

'What could anybody do? I'd just look at him and think, "You are going to die too." I think that about everybody. Just now I remembered us in our holland frocks with scratches on our hands – and then I saw us dying.'

I remembered my own thoughts about those same children, about how lucky they were to have their bellies full of food and I was most curiously ashamed.

'I think,' said Pen, speaking slowly as though deliberating her words, 'that you happen to be one of those people for whom religion, some belief in a future life, is a necessity. What you can't stand, really, is the thought of annihilation. If you could once get a good hold on a belief in the immortality of the soul you wouldn't mind the decay of the body any more.'

Megan turned towards Pen this time.

'I know. I want to be a Catholic.'

'Well, go on, then. Be one. Why not?'

'I don't think I have enough faith.'

Pen hitched one of her pointed shoulders in a fidgety way she had.

'Be something else then. A Baptist, or a Transmigrationist, or a Buchmanite. It's all the same ultimately.'

'But I don't think I have enough even for that.'

'Well, I can't give it to you. You must cultivate it. That is the whole point. Faith, like all other habits of mind, grows with its own practice.'

'I know,' Meg said dolefully. 'That's the trouble. I know you think I'm pretty futile. That's why you say, "Have faith," just like you'd say, "Have an aspirin." You don't sound as though you'd got any yourself.'

'I haven't. But, then, I don't have to. The idea of Penelope Field, who was a child and then a young woman, becoming an old hag and eventually a corpse doesn't raise a qualm in me.'

'You aren't very fond of yourself, are you, Pen?' I asked in a sudden flash of curiosity.

'I haven't much cause to be.'

'Then you think it's self-love?' Megan asked, unoffended.

'Unconsciously, yes. I quite see that it's more difficult for you than for me. You've always been pretty; naturally and rightly you're fond of your body. Watching it fade and become less attractive must be hell for you. That's why I recommend religion.'

'But it isn't only the body, Pen. The mind is blotted out too. All your memories, the good times and the grand people you've known. It makes everything seem so futile. Oh, I know I'm no good at this kind of talk, but to think that even all the love you've known, everything you've felt, everything that makes you *you* is bound for oblivion, that is what is so appalling.'

'What's wrong with it? You've enjoyed the good times and the grand people. You can't ask more than that.'

'Oh, Pen, I can't talk to you. You don't sound human. You understand, don't you, Polly?'

'I begin to,' I said. And my own words frightened me. I pushed away the thought. This was just one of Meg's moods, like the tantrums that she had as a child, which had upset every one in the household so that our nerves were still quivering long after she had recovered.

She had turned and begun to walk away. Pen tossed her bag of blackberries over a bush, and I dropped mine into a clump of nettles. Then we followed her.

'You've forgotten,' Pen began again, patiently, 'that I'm a bit older than you and have had, if I may say so, a rather different kind of life. I'm resigned. You've been a bit late arriving at this stage, I think. Most people get it settled earlier, and either go gay and forget it, or evolve some theory, most suitable to themselves, regarding immortality.'

'No other alternatives?' I said.

'They're the only ones I ever heard of. The only ones that "the Good Book" as Grandmother used to call it, has to offer. Either "Prepare to meet thy God" or "Eat, drink, and be merry".'

'And which,' I asked, 'have you chosen, Pen?'

Pen laughed.

'Once I actually prepared to meet my God, but He didn't like the look of me. Polly, don't you think a drink would be an idea? Come on, then.' She took hold of Megan by the elbow and we began to hurry away into the house as though the brakes had suddenly become haunted.

Going out by the back way to take the dogs into the fields that evening, I noticed that the dustbin lid was tilted. I went to put it straight. But the dustbin was full beyond the brim with bottles and jars. Mary Castle's Eye Lotion, Powder Base, Night and Day and Pore Cream, Petal Powder, Bloom Rouge, Eye Shadow, and a flask three-quarters full of Lotus Blossom perfume.

I fished them out and brushed off the tea-leaves and ashes that clung to them. When I had set them on the shelf in the wood-shed the last rays of light wakened the prisms in the glass again. Too nice, I thought, to throw away so. After all, it was not they who had let Megan down.

Dinner was a ghastly meal, despite Miss Finch's excellent

cooking. I had to make a determined effort not to look at Megan's undecorated face. With that cluster of curls on the brow, with its suggestion of youthfulness, it looked like the face of a child that is frightened of the dark. I wished that I could think of something that would console her. But there just wasn't anything. Mortality is the burden of us all, and if she couldn't bear it unconsciously – as I had done, or carelessly – as Pen did, well, that was just her damned luck! All I could do was to try to provide diversion and keep up a flow of chatter.

Afterwards Pen started the gramophone, and Megan went up to her room to write a letter.

'I do hope,' I said idly to Pen when we were alone, 'that she isn't in the habit of writing that graveyard stuff in letters. She got me properly jacked up with it all this morning. It's the last thing I should expect from her.'

'Is it? Actually, it's so normal as to be pathological. Pretty, romantic-minded women often go gaga that way when their sexual impulses begin to weaken. Either religion or nymphomania gets nine out of ten in the end.'

'Well, nymphomania may be uglier, but it's easier to cope with, I think,' I said. 'Let's hope she chooses that, if choice is inevitable.'

'It doesn't matter much, either way,' said Pen, and it seemed to me that there was just a suggestion of a sigh in her voice. For the first time – perhaps because the events of the last day or two were beginning to have effect upon me – I caught myself wondering what lay behind the cool, hard, impassive front that Pen turned to the world. Her detached attitude towards Megan's state of mind, the way she discussed women's reactions, struck me, for the first time, as being queer. After all, she was a woman herself, not far separated from Megan in age, widely as their lives and experiences had differed. Had she, I caught myself wondering, cultivated her intellectual side until the emotional had withered? Or had she met with some unfortunate experience that had hardened and chilled her? She'd never been pretty, never had vivacity enough to hide the stark fact; and as I looked at her I had a kind of vision of the pale, leggy, clever little girl going determinedly down the years, choosing her work, choosing her attitude, perfecting it, and all the time being conscious of something missing. Perhaps when she said, 'pretty romantic-minded women' in that impersonal analytical way, she was envying them all the time.

But I put that thought away as soon as it was formed. There was no envy in Pen, and, almost I dared have sworn it, no frustration either. Because there was a power in her. What she wanted she would have taken. No doubt of that. Not for the first time I was conscious of shame in comparing my life, my character with hers. My drifting years, my shoddy affairs, my present forlorn hankering after Roger, my love of cash and the things that its possession brought me . . . cheap and unworthy all of them. Ugh! I thought with a mental shrug, Pen always did fire my inferiority complex, being older and so much cleverer. Perhaps I'm still seeing her with the eyes of a schoolgirl. Perhaps she's quite ordinary, really, just a virtuous old maid. Then I was ashamed again. You couldn't class Pen like that.

Megan came down with a coat slung over her shoulders and a couple of letters in her hand.

'Going to walk to the post?' she asked us, and we tore ourselves out of our comfortable chairs to go with her.

'How I used to dread coming up this drive alone,' I said, as we went through the shadow of the laurels.

'So you did,' said Megan. 'And now you don't mind living there all alone. Or do you? Don't you get jittery when the wind howls?'

'Not a bit. Fears are funny things. I can trace mine exactly. It was wolves first, in the shrubbery, and there was a black bear, too, in that corner of the passage by the back stairs. Then they went and I was terribly afraid of burglars, and after that of ghosts. Then, I suppose, I grew up and found real things to fear, and I wasn't afraid of being by myself any more.'

'Real things? What are you afraid of now, Polly?'

'Having teeth out, and being poor,' I said, with prompt truth.

'Fancy,' said Megan. 'Now I go to the dentist's like a lion. And dread my looking-glass. Are you afraid of anything, Pen?'

'Well, yes,' said Pen. 'I am. I'm terrified to death of being afraid, and I bet it gets me into more bother than either of your phobias. If I ever catch myself wondering what will happen if I do this, or say that, or question the wisdom of any of my plans, I just say, "Ah, you're scared." And then I simply have to say it, or do it, whatever it is. And God, what it lands me into sometimes. Simply because I'm scared.'

'How absurd,' said Megan. 'If you really did that you'd be behaving like a lunatic all the time. For instance,' she looked up at the top of the telegraph post to which the letter-box was fixed. 'Would you be afraid to jump from the top of that pole?'

'Yes, naturally.'

'Well, then . . . according to what you said just now, you ought to climb it straight away and throw yourself off it.'

'That isn't so at all,' said Pen, in a reasoning voice. 'It would never occur to me that any useful purpose could be served by doing that, therefore it would never occur to me to do it. But if any purpose could be served, and it did occur to me to do it, and then I felt scared, well, then it would work. Half of me would cry out, "Aha, you're scared," and I should be so terrified that I should do it right away.'

'You wouldn't.'

'I've done worse things than that,' said Pen in a dead way.

'Aren't you going to post those letters?'

Megan separated them and studied the top one in the faint light of the moon.

'Letter for Henry,' she said, and slipped it in. The other she held a moment more, raised it half-way, and then lowered her hand sharply.

'Christ,' she said violently, and the sudden word sounded more like a prayer than an oath, 'I've got the mind of a jellyfish!' She tore the letter across several times, using all her force on the good tough paper, and flung the pieces over the hedge. 'Come on, talk, say something, say anything! You, Polly, why are you afraid of having teeth out?'

Almost hysterical for the first time in my life, I gasped, 'B-b-b-because I've got t-t-twisted roots,' and began to roll about the road, helpless with laughter.

II

First down in the morning, it was I who picked up the letters from the mat and took up, on Megan's tray, the missive that changed, it seemed, her mind from jelly to granite. It had been forwarded twice, that letter, once from a London hotel to Pen's place, and from there to Pedlar's Green.

Pen met me on the stairs; she preferred, she had told me, to breakfast at a table. She said, with a kind of bleak humour, jerking her shoulder towards their room, 'We've had a hell of a night. Turning and tossing and yappering about how one joins the Roman Catholic Church. Would I know? God, it'd be funny if it weren't so beastly pathetic.'

'I know,' I said. 'I'll be down in a minute. Ring for the breakfast, will you?'

In the room that seemed curiously bare without the jars and bottles, Meg scrambled up in the bed when she saw me. She looked grim: hollow-cheeked, hollow-eyed, and frail to a degree. Her eyes fell immediately on the letter, and at once the hollowness and pallor of her face was washed over and drowned by a flood of colour that began at the chiffon frill of her nightgown and rushed up to lose itself in the tangle of her unnetted hair. Her lips parted and her eyes darted over the single page. I watched her. When I withdrew my eyes it was a second too late. She looked up and saw me staring. 'It's from some one I met on the boat,' she said, smiling; but the smile and the words denied our sisterhood. I was a stranger caught staring and the explanation sounded as though I had asked for it. I almost blurted out, 'I wasn't curious. I just wondered if this would cheer you at all.' But, instead, I said, 'Have you got all you want?'

'Yes, thank you,' she said, and the words didn't really apply to the loaded tray.

Megan's post had often been a matter of family interest in those distant years. There would be a letter from some boy who had got her address, and Mother would ask, in a voice that demanded an answer, 'Who is that letter from, Megan?' Once Megan had said, 'From Evie,' with a look that convicted her of lying, and Mother had said, 'I don't believe you. Give it to me.' Megan had looked helplessly at Father, who said, reasonably enough, 'If there's anything in it that your Mother can't read, Meg, Evie is an unsuitable friend for you.' We all waited, tensely. Tears gathered in Meg's eyes and hung on her lashes in a very disarming fashion.

'I am waiting,' said Mother.

Meg bowed before the inevitable.

'That was a lie,' she said. 'It's from a boy.'

'What boy?'

'A boy who sometimes walks to school with me. He's a nice boy, Mother, really. And there's nothing in the letter, but it would . . . it would seem silly if you read it.'

Mother read it. Worse, she read it aloud, in a peculiarly mocking voice. It did sound silly. She intended it to. Megan began to cry in earnest. 'I didn't want him to write to me,' she blubbered. 'I told him not to.'

'And for this,' said Mother, tapping the offending sheet, scrawled all over with boyish writing, 'for *this* you lie to your parents. For this you waste your time at school for which we have to scrape and save the fees. I am pained, surprised, and disgusted at you.'

I regret to say that the rhythm of 'pained, surprised, and disgusted' impressed us more than the import, and we used to express disapproval amongst ourselves in those terms for a long time.

But Megan had other letters. Almost every holiday the scene would be repeated. And Mother always read the letters, and Megan always cried. Then Mother died and the first time that Megan had a letter after that – though of course her letters had been uninspected for some time by then – she looked across to Mother's place at the table and burst into tears. Pen, who happened to be home at the time said, very puzzled, 'But you never *liked* showing them to her, did you?'

And here, after all those years, in the very same house, Megan was holding a letter in her hand, tugging on a dressing-gown and following me down the stairs to the telephone. I heard her asking for a London number as I closed the dining-room door.

I told Pen. 'There's a letter from someone she met on the boat, and she's telephoning now.'

'Aha,' said Pen, crumbling a piece of toast, 'I'm afraid God will have to wait a while longer.'

Megan was down and dressed by the time that I had drained my last cup of coffee. Pen had gone out into the garden.

'Hullo,' I said, 'you have been quick.'

She put on the expression that had gained her Heaven knows how many favours.

'Polly, darling, will you do something for me? Take me into Stoney now, at once, will you?'

'Of course,' I said. 'Are you leaving today?'

She nodded. 'If you don't mind. You said you wouldn't. Only you see – I can't go straight to the station. I did such a fool thing yesterday. You see . . .' she hesitated and traced a pattern on the carpet with the toe of her shoe. 'I got all worked up, and I thought I wouldn't ever bother about anything so trivial as my face again. I put all my stuff in the dustbin. And I wrote that letter, calling off all this other affair. And then I couldn't post it. I'm so *glad* I didn't. Now I must go and arm myself again. Would you think there's a shop in Stoney that has heard of Mary Castle?'

'I doubt it very much. But come with me.'

I led her to the wood-shed and pointed to the shelf.

'Oliver Cromwell was a very sensible bloke,' I said. 'He gave vent to this remarkable statement, "Trust in God and keep your powder dry." You should remember that.'

Megan threw her arms round me and squeezed out all my breath.

'You dear, you darling, you sweet Polly! You've saved my face, as the Chinese say.' She lifted the hem of her skirt and began gathering the bottles into the lap of it. In less than half an hour she came out to me in the garden. The delicate vivid mask of her makeup was on her face again, and the mask of gaiety was on her soul. She twined an arm round my waist and turned me away from the house and fell into step beside me.

'You don't mind, darling, do you, my going, I mean?'

'I shall mind, but I want you to do what you want, of course.'

The mental mask slipped a trifle.

'I don't know what I want, and that's the truth. But I can't stay here, Polly. You see what it does to me, don't you? All that atmosphere of the past and the years . . . and the . . . the innocence of it all. I've tried to get back, to wash it all out. It's no good, Polly. I think about the years till I feel like an ant, and about the space beyond the stars till I'm mad. And the only thing that can save me is a shattering affair, a feeling, a traffic in the flesh. While you're feeling anything you're not finished; and while you can have fun you're not old.'

'And are you going to have fun?'

'Yes,' she said, 'I'm going to have fun.'

'And Henry?' I asked foolishly. I didn't like Henry, but he had a certain soundness and was terribly attached to Megan.

'Oh, Henry,' she said, and her voice was a shrug. 'Henry's all right. But he can't save me any more. All that is like an old coat – nice enough, but no good to keep out the wind. But a fine new coat, a fine new coat, that will keep out the wind.'

'What wind? You're full of parables this morning. What wind?'

And then Megan said a strange thing. 'The wind of the spirit that bloweth where it listeth. And the queer thing is that it blew on *me*. I wonder why. But it was no good. I'm one of the carnally minded – you know about them?'

'No,' I said harshly. 'I didn't have so long a course of Grandmother's Bible reading as you did.'

She ignored the gibe.

'Then you won't remember the scarlet woman of Babylon, whose cup was full of fornication and other abominations. I am she. But oh' – she let go my waist and stretched her arms out from the shoulder, bracing her slim body against the wind – 'it's heavenly to feel something again, to want something. I've been numb for so long. And to think that I've been playing with the idea of being a nun!' She dropped her arms and laughed. 'Come and help me pack, darling. I'd like to catch the two-ten.'

III

'I GUESS I'd better go tomorrow. Work's piling up all this time,' said Pen, as we stood on the platform waiting for Megan's train to pull out.

I said, 'Oh, no, you must stay,' rather absently, for I was looking at Megan. The prospect of pleasure, which simply meant another conquest for her, had made her radiant. The smart little hat with the eye veil that just brushed her nose, the trim town suit and the silver fox fur slung carelessly over one shoulder, the perfume, the good, much-travelled-looking luggage, built up the impression of a woman, well cared for, beautiful, assured, elegant and well-to-do. I thought, I haven't seen you for a long time, and it may be years before I see you again. I may never see you again. And how on earth shall I think of you? Smiling from the first-class carriage? Blubbering amongst the blackberries? Brooding over Time by the fire? Which are you? Which is Megan? Which is my sister?

The guard raised his green flag. We exchanged the last hasty kisses, the last insincere promises about writing regularly. A white-gloved hand waved a handkerchief as the train rounded the bend and Megan had gone.

'I'm afraid she's a trifle cross with me,' said Pen as we reached my car. 'I begged her to wait for a little.'

'Oh, did you? Perhaps I ought to have done, too. I just accepted it when she said she was going. She seemed so much braced – and – and I'm afraid I'm not very moral, Pen.'

'Well, don't sound so apologetic! Neither am I. I'm simply pessimistic, and I think she's just in the state to make a pretty fool of herself.'

'Oh, dear,' I said, 'what a problem it all seems.'

'Simply because she's discovered that she won't live for ever. That's what it amounts to. But, of course, she always was like that, suddenly seeing that two and two were four and never realising that everybody else had known it for ages.'

I looked ahead along the road where the russet and yellow leaves were dancing in the sunshine. And I thought, it's a golden autumn afternoon, and I'm seeing it. There have been hundreds like it, and the people who saw them are dead. There'll be hundreds more and we shan't be here to see them. Hell! I've caught Megan's bug.

'I see what she's driving at in all that talk,' I said.

'So do I,' said Pen, turning her uplifted brow on me. 'But it seems a poor reason for adultery.'

'You don't need a reason for that,' I said, and my words were lighter than my mood.

'I suppose not,' said Pen, and began to talk about something else.

I had been on the verge of asking her then, 'Pen, have you ever been in love?' I felt that if I knew the answer to that I should know something more about her. There might be a story that would explain things. Besides, I really wanted something that would take my mind off Megan. But the moment slipped and I didn't get a chance to ask that impertinent question until after dinner when Miss French had slipped away like an attendant shadow with the coffee tray.

'Pen,' I said, 'have you ever been in love?'

The sound eyebrow went up to match the other, and she gave me that old quizzical look.

'Whatever makes you ask that?'

'I've often wondered,' I said, a little uncomfortably. 'Just as I've often wondered about your face – that accident. Oh, don't tell me if you'd rather not. I suppose you think that curiosity is vulgar. You're never curious, are you? Only . . . it's struck me in these last few days that really . . . we don't know much about one another, do we? And an undertone in my own mind added: of course *you* don't know much about me, and there's a lot, about me and Roger for example, that I'd hate you to know.'

All the same, I did wonder about the 'little accident' to which Pen had attributed the bandaged head and palsy-shaken limbs with which she had faced the assembly at father's funeral. She said now, with a most odd detachment, 'Oh, those scars on my face!' as though they were something quite apart from herself. She slumped lower in the chair and tucked her hands under her folded arms.

'Preparing to tell the story of my life,' she said, jibingly. 'I've never done that before.' But there was a brooding, a remembering look in her eyes that told me that it was coming.

'You wouldn't remember the Andrews, would you? They were kind of relatives of Mother's.'

I shook my head. I had perhaps heard the name before, but it conveyed nothing to me.

'They lived just outside Oxford,' Pen went on, 'and when I went there Mother said I was to go and see them. I did go. I went quite a lot. They were always asking me, and though it wasn't the kind of house that gave you any pleasure to visit I seemed to have to go all the more for that. They were poor, they'd only his pension, he was a retired colonel, and the house was far too big. The fires were always tiny, only just alight, in fact, and in winter it was agony to stay there because the blankets were so thin and scanty. I felt these things more then than I should now. Also the house was full of the most horrible souvenirs, old, odd weapons, beastly brass ware, animals' heads and photographs of people in pith helmets. They'd spent a long time in India – you knew that as soon as you opened the door. It was quite nice in summer, there was a big wild garden with a lot of trees, and the roses all going back to the cabbagy sort. Well, there's the background, as you might say.' Pen paused and twitched her shoulders.

'It was in the war, as you know, and Colonel Andrews' main occupation was putting little flags and tape lines on an enormous map of Europe that hung in a cellar of a room that was called his study. I always had to go and see that the first thing when I went there. I used to have the most awful struggle remembering what it had looked like last time so that I could make some intelligent comparison. Mrs Andrews spent her time trying to save enough sugar from their rations to preserve the currants and things from the garden. One of the girls who used to come out there sometimes with me was diabetic and didn't use sugar, and I'd given it up, so sometimes we used to take some in a bag when we went. That used to please her no end.'

Pen paused and twitched again. I realised that all this had been hedging. I said, 'Hell, Pen, I'm sorry I asked you that silly question. I've stirred up something you'd sooner forget.'

She said, 'It isn't the sort of thing one can forget, my dear,' and went on in a kind of rush.

'One day when I was there they were in the middle of a savage discussion about asking Charlie to stay. Charlie, I gathered, was the son of one of Colonel Andrews' erstwhile fellow officers, he was an orphan and had no people. He'd been wounded, and the old man wanted to ask him there while he recuperated. Mrs Andrews, thinking of food and the servant problem, was equally anxious not to have him. The old man was obstinate, however. I remember he said that day, "There's nothing I wouldn't do for Jim Lawrence's boy. He can come here and run around for a bit with Penelope. They'll be company for one another. Do them both good." He had a kind of simplicity of outlook that you often find in his type. It was very disarming. It made it impossible, for instance, for me to give any hint of what I was thinking, which was that a young officer's idea of doing himself good would not be to run around with a plain earnest student. I knew the kind of girls young officers liked, and the thought of them made me feel leggy and gauche. I'd seen Megan at work!

'However, there I was, roped in as part of the entertainment, and after I'd seen the lad once or twice my shyness wore off, for he was shy too, quiet and young and thin and sunk, utterly sunk in some mood of abstraction to which we had no clue. Throw me a cigarette.' She lifted herself in the chair to reach for the box I held towards her, and cupped her hand round the match, thoughtfully. Once more I had the feeling that the story would end now. It was rather like those old, old films where you were suddenly faced with the words, 'End of Reel 1'.

'At first the old man made a frightful fuss of him, opening his precious port and urging him to drink burgundy because it was "good for the blood". But he cooled off, because, as I discovered, Charlie not only took very little interest in the marvellous map, but showed a marked reluctance to discuss the war in any way. In his more flowery moments Colonel Andrews had been known to refer to it as "this twentieth-century crusade", and that, Charlie told me afterwards, nearly made him sick at the table.

'We, that is Charlie and I, got to know one another very well. It began over a dance that a club I belonged to got up in aid of the hospital funds. He'd taken tickets on condition that I went with him; and though the thing wasn't much in my line I was kind of bound to go in any case. We enjoyed it – about the only thing we ever did, incidentally. He got hold of some whisky and cheered up quite a lot. Oh, dear, the further I go the more explanatory I'm bound to be. There was a doctor at the hospital that I knew through doing a bit of work there, he'd been wounded very early, and had a stiff leg, so he ran a funny little old car, and he'd taught me to drive it. That was a help to him in a way. And on this night, when he knew that I'd come in from the Andrews' house and was going back, he said I might take the thing and drive us home if I could get it back by nine in the morning. He meant well, but it started the whole thing.

'On the way out I went over a rabbit. It squealed, and I got out and went back to see if it was truly dead. Charlie came too. The thing was all squashed, and its insides and blood were all spread out on the road. I was sorry, of course, but not upset. I'd been in the hospital quite a bit, and blood wasn't exactly new to me. Nor to him, I should have thought. So when he went to the side of the road and was violently sick I just thought it was the whisky he'd drunk, or the bump, or something.

'He came back after a moment or so, looking rather

sullen, and I felt a bit awkward – being there, you know – so I began to start the car again, very attentive. Then he said, "I suppose you think I'm drunk. Well, that's where you're wrong. That's the way nasty sights take me, so you can imagine how I enjoy this 'twentieth-century crusade', can't you?" He spoke very truculently, but underneath there was an appeal – bitter, definite, unmistakable. I had a kind of flash of understanding and saw all that that sulky sentence implied. I was probably a bit out of myself too, for somehow I didn't feel shy or constrained any more. I made some sort of sympathetic noise, and then I got the whole flood of it.

'I'd read things, of course, and I'd seen wounded men, but I hadn't begun, until then, to realise what it meant to people who were in it, and who were cursed, through no fault of their own, with queasy stomachs and badly balanced nervous systems. My own were both excellent. Actual physical things had never affected me. But Charlie's talk went straight to a sensitive spot that exists, I suppose, in my imagination only, the spot that used to make me dread that gipsy boy's grave because it could construct out of that mound over a heap of dry bones the terror and the despair that had overtaken him in that last hour of his poor little life. Yes, it was like that. Out of the mound and the bones of the thing that we had got used to, the thing we glibly spoke of as "the war", Charlie evoked for me the living horror of the thing seen from the inside. Can you understand that, Polly?'

'I understand,' I said. 'Go on, what did you do?'

'Very little. What could one do? I know I finished up with my arm round his shoulder and his face pressed into my shoulder – the traditional attitude of defence that comes naturally to women. But the arm couldn't shield him and the shoulder couldn't blind. After a bit I had to start the car again and drive home, and the only thing of comfort I could think of to say was, "You've had a shattering time. You're unstrung. Perhaps you'll feel differently when you're better." Then he laughed, and said, "Not I. I felt this way before ever I saw anything."

'I had an idea that in the morning he would hate himself for having talked as he had done, and me for having listened to him. But no. From that night on he followed me about like a dog. He raked up a rusty old bicycle from somewhere and rode into the town with me, hung about while I was in lectures or at the hospital, and accompanied me home. The Andrews were mildly amused by it all, and teased us rather. Our talk wasn't by any means all raw bones and bloody heads. He was awfully intelligent and had thought and read a lot. I *am* making a long story out of this, am I not? Anyway, I fell for him.

'I suppose that was the only way I could be in love with anybody; I'm not the kind of person who could engage in a jolly flirtation, or who could bear being swept off her feet, as the phrase goes. I want to cherish and comfort and support, odd as that may sound coming from the dried-up old hulk I am now. And all my nice motherly instincts had full play through that long spring and the early summer. And the better I knew him the worse I felt about him. He was so gentle and sensitive. I suppose that sentence is capable of misconstruction, especially nowadays when every one is on the lookout for that kind of thing, and men have to almost parade the hair on their chests to prove that they *are* male. But it wasn't like that at all, though I'm sure he wasn't normal. He was just shattered and utterly incapable of recuperation. And the days fled past until the day came for his examination by the medical board.

'Now I was certain they wouldn't pass him. His whole make-up seemed to me to be so obviously out of gear that I didn't think he'd ever be passed for active service again, although the wound that had sent him home was perfectly healed. The board wasn't in our town, so we rode to the station together in the morning and I propped my bicycle over his by the railings and went on to the platform. He got into the carriage and stood by the door talking to me, and then, just as the train was leaving and I stepped back, he went an awful colour and looked at me, and said, "Penelope, come with me." I tore open the door and scrambled in, just as I was, in an old skirt and jumper, with no hat and no gloves. That doesn't sound strange nowadays, but it looked funny then. They passed him, of course. I realised later that they were turning blind eyes to obvious physical disabilities in that dark hour, so they couldn't be expected to consider nerves.

'And that began the last lap.

'I can't tell you it all. It was like a nightmare. He'd talk about it, his dread of going back, and his worse dread of doing something that would disgrace him for ever, and then he'd break off and talk about something else, striving after the normal, the ordinary the sane.

'I went at last to the colonel. I hoped I'd make him understand. "You know people," I said, "you can do something, pull wires, use influence . . . ". It was awful. He called me a hysterical female, and Charlie a coward. He spoke of Charlie's father who had died the death of a hero. He spoke of England with her back to the wall. He said that if only they'd abolish the age limit . . .

'I fired at the "coward" and said that for Charlie to face one day of modern warfare without cracking was a braver thing for an insensitive block of a diehard to go through a whole death-or-glory campaign. And then the old man surprised me.

' "Young woman," he said, "you talk like a fool. Do you think we weren't frightened? The Afghans torture the wounded, you know, and I've ridden into many an action knowing that if I were wounded and hadn't strength or means to finish off myself I'd die slowly under the knives of the women. I've ridden with a palsy of fear in my knees so that it was hard to hold the horse between them, but I've ridden . . . and forward."

'I was a little ashamed of the things I had said and thought, then. And I could see that there was no help to be hoped for from that quarter.

' "He isn't frightened, he's sick," I said, and came away. After that the colonel hardly spoke to Charlie, and there was no more port or burgundy.

'He – that is, Charlie – didn't sleep much, any more, and we got into the habit of sitting up together, or going for long walks in the night. I think perhaps we were both a little crazy. I know I seduced him – just that. I thought it might take his mind off, but it didn't.

'So the day came nearer, and at last he said there was only one thing to do, stand up again to be shot through the head and pray that the fellow had better aim than the last.

'I said, "*Did* you do that?" He said, "Yes, and I will again." And I thought, what good are you? – even to England with her back against the wall.

' "Do you want to die?" I asked him.

' "It's the only thing that can save me, now." he said.

'And I knew it was true.

'So, to cut short this frightfully long-winded tale, I borrowed the poor little Rover one evening and drove up to the Beacon, which was a highish hill, an escarpment rather, and the road was railed in in places where the drop over the side was sharp and dangerous. We sat at the top and watched the sunset, and we talked a bit. Most of my talk was aimed at delving out new justification for what I was going to do. And I delved out plenty. I thought about watching the sunset for the last time, and that I wouldn't be there tomorrow. I realised that every day is somebody's last one. It's quite an easy thing to accept really. And then I drove down and straight over the edge at a bend. He didn't know anything about it. I had just one wild fear for a moment that the railings were stronger than I thought and weren't going to give way, but they did, and we dropped.

'I didn't wake up for four days, but when I did I was quite clear instantly. There was a nurse in the room and I said to her, "What about the boy who was with me?"

She fenced for a bit and frightened me like hell in case it should all have been wasted, but at last she told me that he was dead when we were found. I went straight to sleep again and slept for the greater part of a week, which shows you what the strain must have been, though I hadn't been conscious of it. And then almost immediately Father died, and I really had to stir myself to get to the funeral. I was all right after that. At least, I hated myself. I can't think why. I'd do it again. And I am not *sorry*. I just hated myself. I wanted to do a kind of penance. Of course I was young.

'The first thing I tried to do, as a kind of atonement, was to leave Oxford and get a job and look after you. But Father had arranged for your future – about as badly as he did everything. And then I heard of the Mary Montague – just starting, short of helpers – made for me. It's good work, and I hate it. The squalor, the regulations, the horrible things you have to see and do. I'm not fitted for it really. I like colour and life and violence and luxury. I like lovely, intelligent people. But I've been there eighteen years, and I shall be there till I die. My God, what an egotistical outburst!'

She broke off abruptly on that note of scorn, reached for a cigarette and lighted it. The flare of the match showed up the scars on the hard thin face, the satirically lifted eyebrow, the deep steady eyes, the beautiful blue eyes of a woman who loved life and violence and colour, and had renounced them all. I thought, so this is what happened to the little girl who used to take prizes at school: this is the thing that Pen has carried about with her all these years. Dear God!

I couldn't say anything at all. If respect and homage and appreciation of a person's sheer character were tangible things that could be made up into a parcel and held out like a present I could have offered Pen a surprising amount. But these things have to be spoken, and I could find no words at all.

Presently she said, flicking away ash, 'I bet Megan's

having a fine time now.'

'Yes,' I said, 'she's hugging the chains of her mortality tonight.'

'Well, that's the only thing to do with chains, you know, Polly.'

I thought suddenly, with a sickening vividness of my chains, desire and lust and hunger for Roger.

'You're right,' I said. 'Have a drink?'

IV

PEN left next morning. I tried to dissuade her, knowing the uselessness of my arguments, even as I uttered them.

'You'll come again, anyway, won't you?' I urged her. 'Come for Christmas.'

Pen smiled. 'Do you think you'll be here at Christmas?' she asked.

'Of course. I'm here for good,' I said.

The little car, the patient donkey of the automobile world, pegged away down the lane, and as I turned from watching it and closed the white gate behind me, a sense of dire enchantment, such as my prosaic mind had never known before, fell upon me. The circle had narrowed ripple by ripple after each departure, and now I was alone. I was alone before that last interview with Miss Finch who, lingering after clearing away my luncheon things, told me that she must leave, the country was getting on her nerves.

'You can go now, at this moment, if you like,' I said with spurious kindness. I gave her a week's wages and hardly noticed her going.

The evening, falling appreciably earlier today than yesterday, came on dull and cold. I built up a huge fire and let in the dogs to sit by it with me. I heard the footsteps of the stockman from the Hall Farm go down the lane. He would be the last person to travel that way tonight. Mrs Pawsey had gone, long ago after laying the table in the dining-room for my meal. I didn't go near it. I sat by the fire and gave myself up to the enchantment that had befallen my peaceful home, my happy life.

Of what was it made? And how had it fallen?

Three days ago I had welcomed them in, those guests who had taken away something that they had not brought, and left at the same time so much behind. I thought about each in turn. And I thought about them not as solid people but as little marionettes, hurrying down their appointed paths under the leaden eyes of the unseeing sky.

Dahlia, my first guest, my foundling, my mascot who had let one part of her, like a black procuress, offer the white Dahlia to Chester Reed for his pleasure. I saw her going down the years, hiding God knew what regrets, losing her looks, going heavily, going gravewards.

I mourned over Dahlia, as she was, and as she would be. And Megan, my pretty sister. Lovely Megan, with her laughter and her bluff; happy Megan with her clothes and her bottles and her men. Megan had come back stricken with a strange disease, and Pedlar's Green had made it worse. 'Saul, Saul, much thinking hath made thee mad.' Who had said that, and why? Just a little thinking had made Megan mad, and like a victim of hydrophobia she had bitten me in passing and now the same madness moved in me. For I could see her, too, moving under the leaden sky, from one diversion to another, from this lover to that, until at last the time for diversion and the time for lovers alike would be gone and Megan must turn towards the grave that she dreaded. Laughing Megan, who had kissed Alf Wicker behind a haystack, was it for this you were made?

And Pen? Ah, surely I could think of Pen with comfort, for Pen feared nothing. As she enjoyed nothing. And I knew then that the measure of our fear is the measure of our enjoyment. We fear to lose what we enjoy. And Pen would not fear death, having been dead these many years. Her very strength had been her undoing. Where weaker people had wept and wrung their hands in the face of what was too strong for them, Pen had acted as though she had been God, or, at least, His deputy. And this strong sad woman had been a little girl who had played at keeping house, and had enjoyed blackberrying, and had sat here by this very fire, munching apples and walnuts on just such a night as this.

What does life give in exchange for what it takes away? I asked. And there was no voice, nor any that answered. Only the wind howled round the house in the way that I remembered; and Block got up and went to the door so purposefully that I had to rise to let him out.

'Make one errand of it,' I said, and drove them all out into the garden.

I did not go back to the fire. I made the round of the house, pressing on lights before me and darkening them behind. I'd loved it so. All my white paper, all my corners and shining spaces. I'd offered it freely to those three women who had passed through it quietly on one certain spot of their different paths and who had left me with this weight of melancholy to grapple with as I could. I hated the house now. I could only think of those children who had banged its doors, played in its corners, laughed, growing every day towards their destiny, beginning even then, and all unconscious of it, to serve their death sentence. I went back to let in the dogs, and we all sat down again by the fire.

'I think I'm going crazy,' I said to the bright eyes in those hairy faces. And the ears pricked at my voice, and the tails stirred lazily. Dear adorable faithful creatures, but there is no comfort in you. Between me and you there is a gulf wider than that which separated Dives from Lazarus. They were both men. Lay your unthinking heads upon your earth-dampened paws and sleep, my friends, you cannot help me now. For I, Polly, Phyllis Field, am the third child.

I have known hardship, and a scrap of success; I have had an affair or two and have been a little in love. Not much, like Megan, not greatly, like Pen, but a little. And I, too, travel down the years under the sky towards certain oblivion. And there I stopped.

Almighty hell, I said to myself, are you going to spoil what days you have because the day comes when you won't know it? You must escape, break this chain, forged of quietude and loneliness and three guests who were unfortunately chosen. Take a drink and get hold of yourself.

So I poured a stiff one and drank it quickly, and another to keep it company. And I said to myself, 'Polly, you need a treat. Your entertainment has been a failure and you're alone in the house. Autumn is here and the wind would drive anyone nutty. What is the most self-indulgent thing you can do yourself?' The answer came with stunning promptitude: 'Ring up Roger Hayward. Remember that letter.'

I remembered it. It had been one of the major surprises of my life. It had been written some time after our break and had done quite a bit of travelling to reach me. It was so essentially Roger's letter that I was forced to admit its sincerity, and for that reason I had preserved it in the inmost flap of my notecase. I took it out now and read it, though I could have repeated it word for word.

'Polly, my dear [it ran], it is some time since you went off huffed or satiated, whichever it was, and I dare say think it odd of me to write to you now. As it happens I've been thinking about you. You know how I loathe introspection, and I know how you loathe sentiment, but something impels me to write this. Perhaps age with its vagaries is overtaking me! Generally, I am relieved at the end of my affairs, but about ours I am sorry. There was just something, I can't say what, in it, and in you, that I haven't found elsewhere. I wish I'd seen that sooner. You've finished with me; but if ever I can do anything for you in any way, if only to while away a dull half-hour, I wish you'd let me know. I'd go a long way and I'd wait a long time to prove that I remember you with much kindliness and some regret.'

Now that was something to have received from Roger Hayward – who should know better than I? And, sitting there with my crazy miserable thoughts for company and the wind howling like a fiend out of hell round the house, the thought of Roger and the sight of his writing was as stimulating to me as – as – well, there just is no comparison.

Roger hates introspection. Roger does things all the time – makes love, eats, drinks, plays games, talks, travels, makes love again. The fact that his legs and his eyesight will one day fail him has never occurred to him. He'll begin to worry about that on the day that they do so. Roger is like I was before this set in. And if I could be with him . . . and never mention these three days – that is important – he could save me.

Never mention these three days. Is that important? Or would he just laugh and say in that lazy voice, 'Well, what can you expect? Shutting yourself away with a lot of introspective women. Come on, Polly, snap out of it.'

But you couldn't dismiss this all as the vapouring of a lot of introspective women. It had been a very real experience. It was concerned with essentials. I knew that. But mine was not a nature to cope with essentials in any other than a practical sense. I couldn't escape either by Megan's road or Pen's.

I must be saved.

I went into the hall and gave Roger's number, and in the interval I thought over what I should say. Oh Roger, my house has been spoiled for me, and my peace shattered. I've had three people I loved here and now I can't think about any of them with any comfort. I've looked out through the safe curtain of this physical being and I've seen us all spinning down the slopes of time like willow leaves on a swift stream. I know it doesn't matter a damn whether I get this call through or not, whether you answer or not, whether I ever see you again or not. There's space beyond the stars that makes you sick with a sense of futility every time you think of it; and every time your heart beats you're a beat nearer the inevitable end. I know that you can be like Pen and accept all these things and still be counted amongst the quick when really you're dead. But, Roger, please, out of your sanity, save mine. Save me from thinking about the menace of the years . . . save me from the horror of impersonal space, save me from seeing people as only God could see them and stay sane. Restore to me the pleasures of the flesh that were given us as a means of blinding the soul. Give me back the kisses, the wine, and the roses that can make all summer in a day that I wouldn't change for the certainty of heaven.

'You're through,' said the voice at the exchange.

'Hullo,' said Roger.

'Hullo,' I said. 'This is Polly, Polly Field. I say, Roger, are you doing anything very much tomorrow?'

A SELECTION OF FINE READING AVAILABLE IN CORGI BOOKS

Novels

☐ 552 08651 7	THE HAND-REARED BOY	Brian W. Aldiss	25p
☐ 552 08889 7	CALIFORNIA GENERATION	Jacqueline Briskin	50p
☐ 552 07938 3	THE NAKED LUNCH	William Burroughs	37½p
☐ 552 08849 8	THE GLASS VIRGIN	Catherine Cookson	40p
☐ 552 08793 9	THE PRETTY BOYS	Simon Cooper	35p
☐ 552 08440 9	THE ANDROMEDA STRAIN	Michael Crichton	35p
☐ 552 08868 4	I KNEW DAISY SMUTEN	ed. Hunter Davies	40p
☐ 552 08125 6	CATCH-22	Joseph Heller	35p
☐ 552 08652 5	THY DAUGHTER'S NAKEDNESS	Myron S. Kauffmann	62½p
☐ 552 08872 2	LADY BLANCHE FARM	Frances Parkinson Keyes	25p
☐ 552 08850 1	FOR INFAMOUS CONDUCT	Derek Lambert	40p
☐ 552 08833 1	HOW FAR TO BETHLEHEM?	Norah Lofts	35p
☐ 552 08888 9	REQUIEM FOR IDOLS	Norah Lofts	25p
☐ 552 08817 X	A FIG FOR VIRTUE	Nan Maynard	30p
☐ 552 08791 2	HAWAII	James A. Michener	75p
☐ 552 08867 6	THE COLLECTION	Paulo Montano	40p
☐ 552 08124 8	LOLITA	Vladimir Nabokov	35p
☐ 552 08853 6	THE MONKEY PULLED HIS HAIR	Frank Norman	30p
☐ 552 08890 0	CRAMBO	Manning O'Brine	35p
☐ 552 08630 4	PRETTY MAIDS ALL IN A ROW	Francis Pollini	40p
☐ 552 07954 5	RUN FOR THE TREES	James S. Rand	30p
☐ 552 08887 0	VIVA RAMIREZ!	James S. Rand	40p
☐ 552 08891 9	THE BALLAD OF THE BELSTONE FOX	David Rook	30p
☐ 552 08597 9	PORTNOY'S COMPLAINT	Philip Roth	40p
☐ 552 08712 2	UHURU	Robert Ruark	50p
☐ 552 08814 5	SOMETHING OF VALUE	Robert Ruark	40p
☐ 552 08794 7	BANEFUL SORCERIES	Joan Sanders	35p
☐ 552 08852 8	SCANDAL'S CHILD	Edmund Schiddel	40p
☐ 552 08372 0	LAST EXIT TO BROOKLYN	Hubert Selby Jr	50p
☐ 552 07807 7	VALLEY OF THE DOLLS	Jacqueline Susann	40p
☐ 552 08532 5	THE LOVE MACHINE	Jacqueline Susann	40p
☐ 552 08217 1	THE CARETAKERS	Dariel Telfer	35p
☐ 552 08091 8	TOPAZ	Leon Uris	40p
☐ 552 08384 4	EXODUS	Leon Uris	40p
☐ 552 08073 X	THE PRACTICE	Stanley Winchester	40p
☐ 552 08481 6	FOREVER AMBER Vol. 1	Kathleen Winsor	35p
☐ 552 08482 4	FOREVER AMBER Vol. 2	Kathleen Winsor	35p
☐ 552 08483 2	THE LOVERS	Kathleen Winsor	35p

War

☐ 552 08738 6	THE BARREN BEACHES OF HELL	Boyd Cochrell	35p
☐ 552 08874 9	SS GENERAL	Sven Hassel	35p

☐ 552 08779 3	ASSIGNMENT: GESTAPO	*Sven Hassel*	35p
☐ 552 08855 2	THE WILLING FLESH	*Willi Heinrich*	35p
☐ 552 08873 0	THE DOOMSDAY SQUAD	*Clark Howard*	25p
☐ 552 08621 5	MEDICAL BLOCK: BUCHENWALD (illustrated)		
		Walter Poller	35p
☐ 552 08757 2	DEFEAT INTO VICTORY	*Field-Marshal Sir William Slim*	40p
☐ 552 08892 7	THE FORTRESS	*Raleigh Trevelyan*	25p
☐ 552 08893 5	THE ENEMY	*Wirt Williams*	30p
☐ 552 08798 X	VIMY! (illustrated)	*Herbert Fairlie Wood*	30p

Romance

☐ 552 08842 0	EDINBURGH EXCURSION	*Lucilla Andrews*	25p
☐ 552 08878 1	NURSE IN THE SUN	*Sheila Brandon*	25p
☐ 552 08784 X	THE DUTIFUL TRADITION	*Kate Norway*	25p
☐ 552 08859 5	THE ROUNDABOUT	*Yvonne Tobitt*	25p
☐ 552 08897 8	IF YOU SPEAK LOVE	*Jean Ure*	25p

Science Fiction

☐ 552 08785 8	I SING THE BODY ELECTRIC	*Ray Bradbury*	35p
☐ 552 08879 X	NEW WRITINGS IN SF-20	ed. *John Carnell*	25p
☐ 552 08860 9	VENUS PLUS X	*Theodore Sturgeon*	25p
☐ 552 08804 8	THE AGE OF THE PUSSYFOOT	*Frederik Pohl*	25p

General

☐ 552 98789 1	INVESTING IN MAPS (illustrated)	*Roger Baynton-Williams*	125p
☐ 552 08768 8	SEX MANNERS FOR OLDER TEENAGERS (illustrated)		
		Robert Chartham	30p
☐ 552 07950 2	SEXUAL BEHAVIOUR	*Dr. Eustace Chesser*	25p
☐ 552 08805 6	WHO DO YOU THINK YOU ARE?	*Dr. Eustace Chesser*	25p
☐ 552 98572 4	NEE DE LA VAGUE (illustrated)	*Lucien Clergue*	105p
☐ 552 08745 9	MAGIC AND MYSTERY IN TIBET	*Alexandra David-Neel*	35p
☐ 552 08800 5	CHARIOTS OF THE GODS? (illustrated)		
		Erich von Daniken	35p
☐ 552 08861 7	THE AUTOBIOGRAPHY OF A SUPER TRAMP		
		W. H. Davies	40p
☐ 552 08677 0	ON THE EDGE OF THE ETHERIC	*Arthur Findlay*	30p
☐ 552 07400 4	MY LIFE AND LOVES	*Frank Harris*	65p
☐ 552 98748 4	MAKING LOVE (Photographs)	*Walter Hartford*	85p
☐ 552 08362 3	A DOCTOR SPEAKS ON SEXUAL EXPRESSION IN MARRIAGE (illustrated)	*Donald W. Hastings, M.D.*	50p
☐ 552 98247 4	THE HISTORY OF THE NUDE IN PHOTOGRAPHY (illustrated)	*Peter Lacey and Anthony La Rotonda*	125p
☐ 552 98345 4	THE ARTIST AND THE NUDE (illustrated)		105p
☐ 552 98862 6	INVESTING IN GEORGIAN GLASS (illustrated)		
		Ward Lloyd	125p
☐ 552 08069 1	THE OTHER VICTORIANS	*Steven Marcus*	50p

☐ 553 08664 9	THE HUMAN ZOO	*Desmond Morris* 35p
☐ 552 08162 0	THE NAKED APE	*Desmond Morris* 30p
☐ 552 08765 3	THE HERMIT	*T. Lobsang Rampa* 30p
☐ 552 08880 3	THE THIRTEENTH CANDLE	*T. Lobsang Rampa* 35p
☐ 552 08630 4	BRUCE TEGNER'S COMPLETE BOOK OF KARATE (illustrated)	*Bruce Tegner* 40p
☐ 552 98479 5	MADEMOISELLE 1+1 (illustrated)	*Marcel Veronese and Jean-Claude Peretz* 105p
☐ 552 08807 2	BIRTH CONTROL NOW AND TOMORROW	*Clive Wood* 30p

Western

☐ 552 08532 4	BLOOD BROTHER	*Elliott Arnold* 40p
☐ 552 08907 9	SUDDEN: TROUBLESHOOTER	*Frederick H. Christian* 25p
☐ 552 08841 2	BAD HOMBRE	*J. T. Edson* 25p
☐ 552 08895 1	NO. 65 GO BACK TO HELL	*J. T. Edson* 25p
☐ 452 08840 4	UNDER THE SWEETWATER RIM	*Louis L'Amour* 25p
☐ 552 08896 X	HOW THE WEST WAS WON	*Louis L'Amour* 30p
☐ 552 08857 9	REVENGE No. 11	*Louis Masterson* 20p
☐ 552 08858 7	STORM OVER SONORA No. 12	*Louis Masterson* 20p
☐ 552 08906 0	SUDDEN: MARSHAL OF LAWLESS	*Oliver Strange* 25p

Crime

☐ 552 08826 9	MURDER WITH MUSHROOMS	*John Creasey* 25p
☐ 552 08875 7	THE TWISTED WIRE	*Richard Falkirk* 25p
☐ 552 08809 9	MADRIGAL	*John Gardner* 25p
☐ 552 08780 7	DEAD MARCH IN THREE KEYS	*Norah Lofts* 25p
☐ 552 08640 1	RED FILE FOR CALLAN	*James Mitchell* 25p
☐ 552 08839 0	TOUCHFEATHER TOO	*Jimmy Sangster* 25p
☐ 552 08894 3	DUCA AND THE MILAN MURDERS	*Giorgio Scerbanenco* 30p
☐ 552 08758 0	SURVIVAL ... ZERO!	*Mickey Spillane* 25p

All these books are available at your bookshop or newsagent; or can be ordered direct from the publisher. Just tick the titles you want and fill in the form below.

CORGI BOOKS, Cash Sales Department, P.O. Box 11, Falmouth, Cornwall.

Please send cheque or postal order. No currency, and allow 5p per book to cover the cost of postage and packing in the U.K., and overseas.

NAME ....

ADDRESS ....

(FEB, 72) ....